Bower House

Bower House

GAIL ELLINGWOOD
Gail Ellingwood

LAVENDER PRESS

Published by Lavender Press
Box 563, Bobcaygeon, Ontario KOM 1A0

This book is a work of fiction. Characters and places are fictitious or are used fictitiously. Any resemblance of persons or locations in the story to actual persons (living or dead) or places is purely coincidental.

Library and Archives Canada Cataloguing in Publication Data

Ellingwood, Gail, 1935–
Bower House / Gail Ellingwood.

ISBN 0-9737062-0-1

I. Title.

PS8609.L54B69 2005 C813'.6 C2004-907164-5

Cover painting by the author
Typeset in Minion by Fox Meadow Creations
Printed in Canada by Métrolitho
PERMANENT PAPER ∞

Dedication

This book is dedicated to Ron, my loving husband of forty-eight years; to our daughter, Cathy Krevs; to our daughter-in-law, Chantal; and to our sons, Peter, Chris and David, all of whom have contributed greatly to its completion.

Author's Note

Since early childhood, I have been an avid reader and amateur artist. It is not surprising then that I became a teacher and taught Grade 3 until my marriage.

My personal taste in reading includes many of the classics, but my first choice could best be described as English-style romance novels. Some of my favourite authors are Jane Austen, Elizabeth Goudge, Georgette Heyer and Miss Read. I have probably read every book written by these authors, and some of them I have read many times.

Of late, I have found it more and more difficult to find a new author that meets my personal taste for cleanliness, modest language and faithful love. As I expressed my feelings to family and friends, I found that I was not alone. At some point, I decided to write my own book using these guidelines.

A story line quickly developed in my mind. Finally, in early 2003, I began to write. The story which you now hold was written by hand in just two weeks. However, I have learned a great deal about book publishing over the past two years. My original manuscript has been edited, re-edited and re-edited again.

I want to give special acknowledgement to Gary Long of Fox Meadow Creations, who guided me so ably through the publication process.

The final result is true to my original story line. But through the generous input of so many people, it has gone from a crude beginning to a story of courage and romance on which I am proud to put my name.

—Gail Ellingwood

Bower House

1

Amy Somerset stirred sleepily as she felt the warm morning sun and the light June breeze on her face. Her dreams were usually pleasant and she woke with a feeling of wellbeing.

Out of habit, she turned to the right to look at her husband's face on his pillow, and her happy thoughts were replaced with a deep feeling of loss. William had died suddenly of a heart attack eight months ago. At times like this, she felt that a part of her had died too.

Will I ever feel whole again? she thought to herself. I must learn to start each day anew and to get out of the house more. Many well-meaning friends had repeated this advice to her, but it had not succeeded in soothing her loneliness.

She could hear the clatter of dishes and the whistling of the tea-kettle coming from the kitchen. Tilly always arrived at seven-thirty in the morning, every day but Sunday. Just as Amy was getting out of bed, there was a tap on her door.

"Good morning, Miss Amy! It's a fine day, and the birds are singing in chorus already. I brought you up a tray with tea and toast and marmalade. Jake has brought round the post and paper too. I thought it would be a nice treat for you to have your breakfast in bed today."

Tilly was such a bright and sunny person and, since William passed away, she had been a great comfort to Amy. She had worked for the family for more than forty years but now the relationship was more one of friendship.

"Now why on earth did you do that, Tilly, when I'm perfectly capable of coming downstairs?"

"You know you need spoiling once in a while," was the reply. "I heard that the parish meeting ran very late last night. You get right back in bed and let me prop up your pillows."

She placed the inviting tray over Amy's knees. Amy thanked her as she left the room singing a hymn that was a favourite of them both.

What Tilly had said was true. The meeting hadn't finished until eleven o'clock thanks to Mrs. Epsom-Smythe, the chair-lady of the Jumble Sale. She insisted on planning everything down to the last detail. She really managed to make a mountain out of a molehill, Amy mused to herself.

She nibbled on her toast, enjoying the marmalade that she and Tilly had made a few months before.

She looked at the lone envelope and knew that it was another bill. She was going to have to go over her budget once more. What am I to do? she thought, with tears in her eyes. William had always done the household accounts, and now she found it very difficult to work things out. At least the house had been inherited from her parents, and the car was also debt-free.

Amy finally got up and took a refreshing bath. She decided to wear a summery dress and sandals. As she looked at herself in the mirror, she had to admit that she was still a little thin. She also noticed a few more grey hairs on the sides of her blonde curls ("silver wings" she called them). All in all, she felt younger than her fifty-eight years.

As she reached the bottom of the stairs, the telephone on the hall table rang. She set the tray down on the table and picked up the receiver.

"Hello," she said, wondering who was calling so early on a Monday.

"Mother, it's Barbara, darling. How are you getting along?" She seemed rather excited.

"Just fine, dear," answered Amy. "It's such a lovely warm morning. Tilly treated me to breakfast in bed and now I'm planning to drive to the village to do some marketing."

"Mother, Jeffery is being sent to Paris on business and has asked me to go with him, but we can't bring the children. Is there any chance that you could keep them with you for two weeks starting this Saturday? We had thought of asking you to come up to London but decided that it would be easier for you to be in your own home, and of course the children will enjoy an early start on their summer holiday. I've cleared with their teachers that this would be acceptable, as they are both very good students."

Amy thought quickly and replied: "I would love to have them visit with me dear, if you don't think that they would find it too quiet here."

"You know they adore you, Mother, and you're so good with them. They love visiting at Bower House. Perhaps, you might take them down to the seashore. A picnic by the shore is one of their favourite outings, just as it always was mine."

"Well, fine then dear," Amy replied, still not very sure.

"Would it be all right if we brought them down on Saturday?" Barbara asked eagerly.

"Yes, yes, that would be perfect," answered Amy. "Mrs. Bromfield, our neighbour, has two children that are about the same ages. Also, a pair of sweet five-year-old twins and their parents moved into Mulberry Cottage down the road a few months ago. I guess there will be plenty of children around for them to play with."

"Well, I'm sure that it'll be fun for them. Shall we say two o'clock on Saturday then Mother? Are you sure these arrangements will be agreeable and not too overwhelming?" asked Barbara anxiously.

"No, no. As a matter of fact, I shall quite look forward to it all. You know how I love my grandchildren. Can you and Jeffery stay for tea on Saturday?"

"Yes, that would be lovely, and thanks so much, Mother. I'm quite excited about this trip. Goodbye, see you on Saturday."

Amy carried the tray out to the kitchen and said to Tilly: "That was Barbara on the phone. We have the children coming as house guests for two weeks starting Saturday while their parents are away in France. Jeffery has business and Barbara is going with him."

"My, my," said Tilly. "Are you sure that you can take on those two young ones? I guess eleven and twelve aren't that young, but they are a busy pair."

"Well, it seemed to be all settled before I could catch my breath," Amy replied, "but it will be good for me to be thinking of someone besides myself."

Tilly replied, patting her on the shoulder: "We still have the Jumble Sale to get through on Thursday. Are you going to look up in the attic today for items to sell? Shall I begin preparing the spare bedrooms for the children?"

"Yes. Thank you. But first, I must do the marketing at the grocer's in Ferndene. On the way, I'll stop at Mulberry Cottage and talk to Jane. Maybe she and the twins would like to join us on a picnic when Stephanie and George are here. Do you have the grocery list that we made up, Tilly? We're going to have to make some substantial additions to provide for tea on Saturday and to satisfy the children's hearty appetites."

They talked about menus and a long list resulted. Tilly said: "While you're gone, I'm going to prepare a lovely meat and potato pie for your lunch, with a fresh green salad and a bit of fruit pudding."

"You're certainly spoiling me, and still trying to fatten me up," Amy replied with a laugh and a hug. "And thank you again for that luxurious breakfast in bed."

She went out the front door and down the flagstone path. There were clematis and rose buds on the arched bower. She sniffed the air, appreciating the sweet scents.

As she looked back, she thought, what a blessing to be the third generation to live in this beautiful home.

Bower House was of Georgian style, constructed of local stone that had a slightly pinkish hue. It was a two-storey, centre-hall plan with a large oak door and fluted pillars supporting an arched roof over the entry. There were two bow windows on the ground floor and divided windows upstairs. The mature landscaping gave the house an appearance of belonging and permanence.

It had originally been the home of her father's parents and was willed to her father when Amy was only ten years old. She had spent most of her growing-up years here and then returned for good when William took ill three years ago.

She had left while attending business college and, on graduation, moved to London to accept a secretarial position in the offices of Carstairs and Carstairs, Barristers and Solicitors. Within a few years, she became the private secretary of William Somerset who was an up-and-coming solicitor, and soon, a partner in the firm.

She recalled, with a few tears and a pang in her heart how they had been attracted to one another, gradually fallen in love, and married. Their only child, Barbara, had been born just one year later.

They lived all their married life in a lovely and spacious town house, which they rented in central London. Amy had stayed at home to raise her daughter, but when Barbara was eighteen years old, she returned to her job as William's secretary.

William had been a very serious and hard-working man, but also gentle and loveable. He was fiercely loyal to his clients, and Amy believed that many people took advantage of his generous nature, which adversely affected both his health and his earning power.

When Amy's parents passed away five years ago (both in the same year), she and William refused to even consider selling Bower House. They kept it as a weekend retreat from the bustle of the city, and made plans to retire there one day when his career should come to an end. In the meantime, faithful Tilly and her competent husband, Walter, kept the property in prime condition.

Amy and William's decision to keep the house had proven to be very astute financially, but more importantly, Amy had returned to her roots and she hoped to live out her remaining days in these familiar surroundings.

She soon reached Mulberry Cottage and there was Jane Barnaby sweeping her front steps. Her twins ran and hid behind their mother's skirts. They were darling children; both had blonde, curly hair and blue eyes. One was a very feminine little girl, Trudy; and the other, a sturdy little boy, Tommy.

"Hello everyone!" called Amy, smiling at them.

"Oh, hello Amy," answered Jane. "I was so intent on sweeping, I didn't hear you drive up."

"How is everyone today?" Amy asked, looking at the proud mother.

"Very well. We decided to go outside on this lovely day."

"I just heard from my daughter who asked me to entertain her children for two weeks while she and her husband are away. I think that you met my grandchildren on an earlier visit."

"Oh yes, I remember them well," said Jane, "such well-behaved children."

"Well, I was wondering if we could get together for a picnic next Tuesday at the seashore if the weather is nice."

"We'd love to do that," Jane responded. "I'm always looking for things to do with the children. They adore going to the seashore."

"Lovely then," said Amy. "I'll give you a call on Monday and we'll make our plans. Goodbye for now."

At the grocer's, Amy ran into Mrs. Epsom-Smythe, who said in her booming voice: "Hello again, my dear!" The voice certainly matched her appearance. Her severe haircut and trouser suits always seemed to give her a manly appearance.

"I hope that you will have all of your items ready for Wednesday morning at nine-thirty so we can get everything sorted and priced," she said.

"Oh yes, yes," replied Amy. "I'm going through my things this very afternoon."

"See you have my groceries delivered shortly, Davis," bawled Mrs. Epsom-Smythe with a curt nod of her head. "Goodbye, Amy. See you on Wednesday." And with that, she marched out of the store.

"That woman!" said Mr. Davis with a shake of his head. "My wife and I call her 'the Sergeant'. Did you want some boxes for the Jumble Sale, Mrs. Somerset? I can drop them off tomorrow morning."

"I would appreciate that, Mr. Davis," said Amy.

She put her things in the basket as he totalled them up, and then she paid for them. I shop carefully, she thought to herself, and yet it still seems that there is too much money flying out of my purse.

As she drove home, she kept thinking about her vegetable garden and was happy that Walter had been able to expand it for her. He was so good at that.

That afternoon, she found many items in the attic for the sale. There were several well-aged vases and pots, which would be quite attractive when filled with flowers and ivies. She also found old photos, which might not be saleable, but the antique frames certainly would be. In addition, there were some old board games, some of which she put in the sale but others she set aside to play with the grandchildren.

With these items, she thought to herself, my booth should be quite attractive to buyers.

On Wednesday morning, she drove to the church hall and arrived promptly at nine-thirty with all her items in three boxes. Her prices were written down, but she still needed approval from Mrs. Epsom-Smythe.

Amy's friend, Vivian Langford, the doctor's wife, spoke to her in a whisper: "My baked goods are here and more are coming tomorrow morning. I hope they pass the Sergeant's approval."

(There was that name again!) Vivian had a distinct twinkle in her blue eyes that indicated she didn't really care.

Just then, Mrs. Epsom-Smythe said in her usual loud voice: "Now ladies, please put your things on the appropriate tables while I go around and check on them. Mrs. Langford, would you be my assistant please while we decide on prices? I will give out tickets to put on your items."

Surprisingly, this was all completed in an hour and a half and all the ladies were asked to return on Thursday morning at nine-thirty to prepare the final touches for the Ferndene Ladies' Institute Annual Jumble Sale.

"Would you like to go to the Fuchsia Tearoom for a few minutes, Amy?" asked Vivian after they had finished. "That was exhausting."

"Certainly, I wouldn't mind at all." A few other ladies had also found the need for a refreshing cup of tea.

"I'll be glad when this is over," said Vivian, shaking her grey curls in youthful fashion. "I'm really worn out."

"How is your husband these days?" asked Amy.

"Well, Jim's practice is booming. He's had three deliveries this week alone, and all baby boys. Isn't that strange?"

They chatted on over their tea and finally said goodbye to each other.

The next day, Amy was up early, with Tilly insisting on her eating an egg with her toast.

Amy set up her booth, arranging her items in an appealing manner, and displaying the price tags prominently. Of course, Mrs. Epsom-Smythe was here, there and everywhere before the doors opened at ten-thirty.

There was a rush of people through the door and you could feel the charged atmosphere immediately. Amy was quite surprised by the number of persons gathered around her table. In less than an hour, it was completely cleared.

She blinked a few times to clear her whirling head and saw Vivian doing the same. She had just been through a similar experience, and they smiled happily at each other. They counted up the money and turned it in to the treasurer. With weary feet, Amy went home to put her legs up and to have an early lunch.

The next morning, she and Tilly finished preparing the house for the grandchildren's visit. Tilly had washed and ironed the white cotton curtains in the children's rooms and hung the bedspreads out to air on the line. The rooms smelled sweet with fresh balmy air flowing through the open windows.

The small carpets in each room had been hand-made by Amy's grandmother in a tapestry of colours. There were botanical pictures on the walls done in pastel-watercolour that Amy herself had painted many years ago. Fresh flowers from the garden had also been placed in each room.

Tilly did some baking including the gingerbread cookies that the children had loved since they were little.

"Tomorrow morning, I'll bake some tea cakes for the weekend," she said, "and also some things for dinners."

At noon, Mrs. Epsom-Smythe called to say that the sale had raised four hundred and twenty-one pounds, with Amy's booth selling over sixty pounds worth. She was calling each woman to offer her congratulations.

Amy went back to the kitchen and told Tilly, adding that:

“Mrs. Epsom-Smythe might be very bossy, but she has done a wonderful job and, if ‘Sergeant’ describes her, then at least she is a good one.”

They both had a hearty laugh over that.

2

Saturday came all too soon, and of course Barbara and her family were there promptly at two o'clock. The children bounded out of the car and ran up to their grandmother, hugging and kissing her, and nearly toppling her over.

"Oh, Grandmother, this is going to be an amazing vacation, isn't it?" said Stephanie and George in unison.

Barbara and Jeffery came along, smiling. Barbara said: "Be careful now; you're going to knock Grandmother down. Hello, Mother dear. You always manage to look so young. I think that this house agrees with you. The garden is looking charming."

"Hello, Amy," said Jeffery, looking slightly sheepish. "I hope we're not putting you out too much by asking you to keep our two rascals."

Amy laughed and hugged both of the children again. "Never," she said. "We shall have a marvellous time together."

As the three feminine faces shone up at him, Jeffery was struck by the obvious resemblance of one to the other. Amy's hair was still mostly blonde, with greying temples; his wife was starting to think about touching hers up; but his daughter's blonde hair shone with youth's glowing locks. All had twinkling blue eyes, but Amy's showed the maturity of a challenging life well lived.

"Well, don't just stand about," she said. "Let's go into the house. Jeffery and George, you can take the luggage upstairs to the two guest bedrooms."

"Can we look around outside first?" asked Barbara. "We've been cooped up in the stuffy old car and I wouldn't mind breathing some of this glorious country air."

They walked around admiring the roses and clematis coming out on the arch and followed the flagstone path to the back patio.

"Mother, you've expanded the vegetable garden this year," commented Barbara.

"Tilly's husband Walter did it for me; I thought it would be so convenient to have more vegetables right outside my door, and also it would save mowing so much grass," replied Amy.

"Roses were always Daddy's passion, I remember," said Barbara with a catch in her voice. "They look so healthy in that circular bed."

"I have Walter here once a week to help out," replied Amy shakily. "He has such a green thumb and Tilly is very proud of him."

The children came out the patio doors saying: "Grandmother, we feel just like grown-up guests. There are flower bouquets in our rooms and everything looks lovely!"

Amy laughed. "You're growing so fast; you'll soon be grown-ups. You're almost as tall as I am, George. Let's go inside for a few minutes and have a nice chat; I haven't seen you since Easter."

As they went into the bright, long living room with its bow

window, Barbara admired it anew. It was a small but elegant house. On the other side of the central hall was the very pretty dining room with its own bow window. A book-lined library was set in behind it with an arched doorway to the garden. There were four bedrooms upstairs and a second bath. The large kitchen was an extension of the central hallway and had the latest appliances.

When the house was purchased, Amy's grandmother had loved antiques, but her husband would not allow any chairs that were not comfortable. Amy's mother maintained Bower House very well and Amy, of course, had inherited her mother's good taste and made few changes.

Amy spoke, jerking Barbara out of her musings. "Barbara dear, Tilly has made the children's favourite gingerbread cookies and iced cake for tea. Just tell me when you want it served before you head back."

"Oh, that sounds wonderful, Mother," replied Barbara. "You know how the children adore those cookies. By the way, how is Tilly?"

"Just her happy, healthy self, as usual. I'm grateful to have her here. In fact, I couldn't do without her. She spoils me, though, and we do have a few laughs; she has such a sense of humour."

With that, they decided to have an early tea on the terrace and lounged about on the deck chairs. They all helped to clean up, and Barbara and Jeffery left amidst tears and goodbyes, promises to call the children and to send postcards and "to be good for Grandmother." The children went upstairs to put away their clothes and then the three went to the village for a walk.

Amy had a lovely chicken dish for dinner that Tilly had made and just needed to be heated. There was fresh lettuce from the garden topped with her secret dressing. The children went to bed fairly early and were given a kiss and hug from Grandmother.

"Now, don't get up until you hear me downstairs putting on the kettle, will you? Church service is at ten-thirty so we have lots of time to get ready. Good night, dears."

Before getting into her own bed, Amy said a little prayer that all would go well during the children's visit.

After a good breakfast of eggs, sausages and toast, everyone washed up and got ready for the service. They had decided to walk to St. Boniface on another glorious day. The children were nicely dressed, a sure sign that their mother had given them a lecture on how to behave and what to do. Amy smiled to herself, knowing that they were being brought up just as she had brought up her own child.

The Vicar was fairly young, so his sermon was such that the children seemed interested and did not squirm. On the way out of church, Amy introduced her grandchildren to the Vicar and to several of her friends, feeling quite proud as she did so.

As they were heading home, the children asked if they could run the rest of the way. Amy agreed, realizing that they needed to release some of their pent-up energy. As she reached the house, she saw them sitting on a bench at the front door with George dabbing at his knee with his handkerchief.

"Well, what has happened dear?" asked Amy anxiously.

"I tripped on a root and fell down and scraped my knee. It's just bleeding a bit," replied George with a worried frown.

"Let me see it, dear," said Amy as she helped him into the house. "We must first of all clean it up and then see how bad it is." Stephanie was right beside her brother. She had told her grandmother that she was going to be a nurse like her mother when she grew up. George limped along into the kitchen and sat in a chair. His handkerchief had just a few spots of blood on it.

Amy gently cleaned the wound with a dampened tea towel and removed any gravel that seemed to be there. Stephanie handed her the disinfectant, which she swabbed on the cut.

"Thank you, Grandmother," said George, looking at his wound carefully.

Amy announced: "Now I shall get our mid-day meal ready if you two will set the table in the dining room, please." A light shower forced them to stay indoors, so they played board games with much hilarity.

Tilly was hugged and kissed in welcome in the morning. She was all smiles and laughter to have these young people visiting. She served them eggs and sausages, toast and hot chocolate in the dining room.

"I know how hungry you two can get and this will set you up for the day."

Amy watched contentedly as they ate up everything with wonderful appetites of the young. They took their dishes out to the kitchen and asked Tilly politely if they could help clean up.

"We made our own beds and straightened up our rooms. Mother said we were not to be a burden on everyone," said George.

"Now you two young scamps get outside in the good fresh air and enjoy yourselves. I've got all morning to do these dishes.

You have said thank you enough and I can tell by your clean plates that you enjoyed your breakfast."

The children asked if they could go into the "forest" to explore. Since it was only a small wood lot, Amy let them go.

"Perhaps, we can ask the grocer to send up a few things this morning, Tilly," she said, realizing that she had under-estimated the children's appetites. They made a short list, deciding on a cheese soufflé for an economical meal.

"A fresh loaf of bread from the baker's would be nice too," added Amy, "and some more milk. Also, I promised to call Jane today to see if they would like to get together for a picnic tomorrow. But first, we must talk about a menu."

She called Jane who was very enthused about the picnic by the sea, and soon their plans were made.

A few minutes before lunch, George and Stephanie came running in the back door all hot and a little mud-streaked.

"Grandmother, we met the sweetest pair of twins in the forest. They had found a baby bird that had fallen out if its nest and was hopping about, chirping and chirping."

"I climbed the tree and put it back. I hope it doesn't fall out again," said George. "I'm afraid we all got a little dirty looking for the bird; it kept hiding under leaves."

"Well, I'm glad that you found it," said Amy. "Why don't you go upstairs and wash up and get ready for lunch. It will be ready shortly."

At lunch, she told them about the lovely picnic planned for tomorrow and they chattered away happily about what they would do. In the afternoon, it became very hot and sultry, so instead of playing outside they decided just to talk and drink lemonade on the terrace in the shade.

Amy expressed her pride that the children were doing well

in school. Stephanie replied that she had to work hard to keep her marks up, unlike George who seemed to find school easy. "I have to get good marks so I can be a nurse, Grandmother," she said.

George said: "For now, I enjoy sport a lot, but Father and Grandfather seem to be after me lately about either becoming a doctor or a lawyer, and I don't know what I want to do." Jeffery's father was a doctor, so of course since Jeffery had not become one, he had high hopes for his grandson.

"Well, if you want your Grandmother's advice, you have a ways to go yet before you have to decide. Meanwhile, keep doing the best you can, work hard to get good marks, enjoy your sport, and things will fall into place for you. Just remember that everyone loves you and wants what is best for you.

"Have some more lemonade, dears, and I'll get us a nice tea tray. Why don't we just stay here and enjoy it?"

George got up and gave his Grandmother a hug. "You've made me feel much better, Grandmother."

3

The children were up early on Tuesday morning looking out the door and declaring how perfect the weather was for a picnic.

Right after breakfast, they went upstairs and found their bathing suits and some towels. Amy told them to look in the shed for the pails and shovels. She and Tilly packed up the sandwiches, cookies, fruit and lemonade as well as a rug. Amy put it all in the car.

As they arrived at Mulberry Cottage, Jane and the twins were just getting everything into their car, and were soon ready too. It was only a half-hour drive to the sea and they found a favourite swimming cove that was well protected and safe. The perfect spot was found—half shade and half sun and near the water. Everyone was satisfied. The children immediately went to the edge of the water with Jane hovering over her twins like a mother hen.

There was much splashing, screaming and laughing and all the children were wet in no time. Soon they all felt hungry and decided that it was time for lunch, so everyone flopped down on the rugs and started to eat their picnic.

"Everything is just scrumptious, Grandmother," said George. "We're having so much fun."

After lunch, the picnic gear was packed in the baskets and the children went back to the water again. At about three o'clock, the twins, Tommy and Trudy started throwing sand at each other, and finally Tommy pushed his sister down in the water. She came up sputtering and crying, as Jane rushed over to separate the two. "Come and sit down, both of you, right now. I'm afraid you're both getting tired, so our picnic is over."

Stephanie, George and Amy had to hide their smiles. The twins did look like little wet puppies. Everyone dried off and the picnic things were loaded into the cars.

"I'm so sorry," apologized Jane. "I hope my children didn't spoil everything. I will have to give them a warm bath and a hair wash when we get home. Thank heavens they go to school in September, if we all live that long."

Amy and the children waved goodbye to the little family, not admitting of course, that they were tired too. They also had warm baths when they got home. A strong wind came up after dinner and Amy closed up the shutters.

"I think we're going to have a storm tonight," she predicted.

Sure enough, shortly after midnight, Amy was awakened by a loud crash of thunder. The next moment her bedroom door opened and there, in a flash of lightning, she saw Stephanie.

"Oh Grandmother, I don't like all this noise. The lightning and thunder scare me."

"Come here, darling," Amy said, as she moved over in bed. "Stay here with me until it's over." She had forgotten how Stephanie had always disliked storms since she was very little.

"I guess I'm not as big as I think, Grandmother," she said, with a quiver in her voice. They huddled together until the worst of the storm finally passed away and Stephanie felt safe about returning to her own bed.

The next morning, George was dumbfounded when they told him about the storm. He hadn't heard a thing.

Dorothy Bromfield called that morning to tell Amy that her two children had the day off from school. Would Amy's grandchildren enjoy playing tennis or swimming? She had a pool and a tennis court and said that there were always extra rackets and balls about.

Amy asked the children, who of course said "yes."

She took them over to meet the Bromfields. Trixie was the same age as Stephanie—eleven—and Alistair was twelve, the same as George. Dorothy and her husband, Brian, a businessman in London, were prominent citizens of Ferndene. She was a large woman and very kind, and did work for the Women's Institute as the treasurer.

The children were all soon active, playing tennis and swimming in the pool, and very much enjoying one another's company.

On the coming Sunday, there was to be a church fair and supper. This was looked forward to by the whole community. There was to be a small ferris wheel and games for the children and also contests for the best canning, pickling, pies, cakes, etc. I hope that Tilly and I will win for our marmalade again, thought Amy to herself.

Amy invited the two Bromfield children for tea and ice cream after school on Friday to celebrate their last day of classes. Afterwards, they decided to practice for the races that would be a part of Sunday's fair, especially the three-legged race. George, of course, took charge and started counting after they had tied one leg to the other. The girls were racing against the boys.

"Go slowly at first and get a rhythm going," he advised. It seemed to be the perfect approach and soon they were laughing themselves silly, but making good headway. Amy watched from her lounge chair, giving encouragement and laughing aloud. Finally, they flopped down on the grass, too hot to carry on, so Amy served cold lemonade and biscuits to the group.

After Trixie and Alistair went home, Amy said to George and Stephanie: "You're all going to be very good in Sunday's races. George, you make a good captain."

The four children were allowed to go to town together on Saturday to see a horror movie. On returning, Stephanie reported: "It was just gruesome, Grandmother, but we still loved it. We also stopped for ice cream after the movie."

"The girls were sure scared when the giant spider came out," scoffed George. Stephanie gave him a punch and Amy had to scold her.

Sunday was a cool but sunny day with white fluffy clouds scudding across the sky. A slight breeze made the trees wave back and forth in a happy dance. The children were dancing about too, being very excited about the fair.

They went to church in the morning and Amy could see several parents trying to keep their children still. She herself had to give a couple of stern looks to her own grandchildren.

At two o'clock, they went back to the church grounds to attend the fair.

Stephanie and George found Trixie and Alistair, and prepared for the three-legged race. The starter pointed to the finish line further down the grass and all the family members came to watch. The starting gun went off and Amy's two were behind a little but, by keeping a steady beat, they passed the others, some of whom had fallen down laughing. The two pairs were the winners—Stephanie and Trixie, and George and Alistair. They yelled in triumph amidst much clapping, and happily accepted a red ribbon each for first prize.

Amy and the Bromfields both congratulated them and the children were sent off to enjoy the ferris wheel.

Now came the judging of the canning and pickling competition. Tilly and Amy were especially nervous about their marmalade when they found out Mrs. Epsom-Smythe had also entered hers. After a few suspenseful minutes of tasting by the three judges, they found Tilly and Amy's the best and awarded first prize red ribbons to them.

Mrs. Epsom-Smythe had entered her chutney in the contest for that category. After much talk among themselves, the judges decided that her chutney was best and she was very pleased to accept the red ribbon with much humility and a smile for all.

The buffet dinner was the grand finale to the day and everyone was filled to groaning capacity. All were hard put to do justice to the many pies and cakes set out for dessert, even George with his enormous appetite.

Amy and the children went home happily and decided to have nothing for dinner but tea or hot chocolate and biscuits. They all put their ribbons on the hall table, and congratulated each other before heading off to bed.

"We knew you and Tilly would win a prize for your marmalade," said Stephanie. "It should have won first, second and third prize."

Dorothy Bromfield called early on Tuesday morning to ask everyone for lunch. The children could also play tennis or have a swim. "Just a few more days and your grandchildren will be going home. They have certainly been wonderful companions for my two children."

Lunch was at one o'clock, and they tried to be punctual. It was very pleasant on the patio and the congenial group enjoyed the delicious food. The gardens were at their very best—truly lovely.

Just as they were eating their cakes, a large bushy-looking dog came running across the lawn towards the group. It headed for the side table and, with one bounding leap, grabbed some of the cakes in his large mouth and ran off.

"Mercy me!" screamed Mrs. Bromfield. "That dratted dog of Mr. Copperfield's is always running here and there—why isn't it in their yard? Boys, try to catch him if you can."

The dog thought it was a lovely game of tag, and was about to try a second run at the cakes when its owner came running around the hedge calling for "Napoleon" to return at once.

Mrs. Bromfield immediately began giving Mr. Copperfield a good piece of her mind about dogs being allowed to run loose like that. To add to her consternation, Napoleon jumped into the pool and had a good swim to cool off after all its exertions.

"If that dog of yours isn't out of my yard in five minutes, I will call the dogcatcher and the police!" she spluttered, waving her hands.

At that, the dog bounded up to its owner, and gave a mighty shake, splattering water in all directions, especially on Mrs. Bromfield. Luckily, its owner grabbed the collar and quickly led "the animal" off the property.

"Well!" she said, still bristling with outrage. "Will you excuse me for a few minutes while I straighten myself up? I will have Janet bring out some fresh cakes and tea."

Amy and the children were wondering if the scene they had just witnessed could have happened in less than five minutes and each was trying not to look at the other for fear of disgracing themselves by laughing.

The children stayed for a while after lunch playing tennis. Amy tried to talk about this and that to distract her hostess and calm her down. They finally left about three o'clock. As soon as they got into the car, they started to giggle, each recounting the funny things that had happened.

"Now stop it until we get home, you two," pleaded Amy. "I can hardly see to drive with these streaming eyes."

All through the evening, one seemed to set the others off laughing again until they could laugh no more.

4

They walked into Ferndene after lunch one day to do a bit more marketing and Amy treated them both to ice cream at the tearoom.

"I was glad to hear from Mummy last Saturday," remarked Stephanie. "They'll be here for tea this Saturday. The time has gone by quickly and we've had a wonderful time, haven't we, George?" She added, "I loved the postcards from Paris."

George said: "We have had our own adventures too, Grandmother. Do you think we might go on another picnic? That's our favourite thing to do."

"That will depend on the weather predictions," Amy answered. "I would enjoy a picnic too."

"Do you think Tilly might come?" asked Stephanie. "She has been so good to us."

"How thoughtful you are, child," said Amy with a smile. "We'll call her tonight and coax her to come along."

As they wandered back to Bower House, the afternoon sun

shone on the pink stone of her lovely home. The clematis and roses were now in full bloom and the stone wall along the front was covered in ivy with groups of flowers nodding in front of it.

How welcoming, Amy thought.

They had a hearty tea around five, being too full of ice cream to eat anything earlier. Fresh scones and jam and boiled eggs seemed enough to keep everyone until morning. Amy called Tilly and invited her to the picnic.

The next day, the children were up early. The radio had told them it was to be a fine day. They were anxious to greet Tilly and to share their enthusiasm for the picnic.

"Just don't expect to see me in a bathing suit," Tilly laughed. "All my bulges will show up." Being rather thin for sixty-five, this was quite a joke, and they all had a good chuckle over it.

Tilly said to Amy: "Is it true that I'm being dragged on this picnic? Do you really want me to come?"

"Of course, we do. The children decided it would be a fun party and also a way of thanking you for all you've done for them."

"We'll get everything ready, Tilly, if only you'll make up some more of your gingerbread cookies, please," pleaded Stephanie. "We don't have much time left."

George added: "We'll go to the village this morning to get the picnic supplies with you, Grandmother."

"Those two are such thoughtful dears. I hope you don't mind my coming with you. I haven't been on a picnic in two or three years. Walter is always working, but we did take our own grandchildren on a picnic when we went for a visit. I also told them that they weren't going to see me in a bathing suit," Tilly added.

Amy laughed. "It hasn't been too bad having them here. They are sweet, lovely children aren't they?"

"Well, they surely liven things up and I am sure they haven't had time to think much about missing their parents."

With that, Amy started to prepare a list for shopping, leaving space for the children to make up their menu.

Another bill had arrived in the mail this morning—this time for her taxes.

Oh dear, she thought to herself, I'm just going to have to sit down next week and go over my ledgers. Where else can I cut corners? I would hate to cut down on the days that Tilly comes for she has been a part of this family for so many years.

Amy watched her grandchildren and noticed the rosy glow the children had now, whereas they had looked rather pale when they arrived.

"Only fifteen more minutes and we're allowed to go into the kitchen and make up the picnic," said George. "We have our bathing suits, towels, shovels and pails."

Stephanie added: "I wish Mummy would let us do more things like this. We love you, Grandmother. We have had such a good time, haven't we George?" With that, they both gave her another hug.

Tilly had her own rug, a large sunhat and a towel. "I just thought I might put my toes in the water seeing as it's going to be a warm day."

Soon all was ready, the children re-assuring Tilly that they had straightened up the kitchen so well she wouldn't even know that they had been working there.

They piled everything into the car and the children started singing "Row-row-row your boat" with Tilly getting totally mixed up and causing much laughter.

They chose their favourite site and Stephanie and George were soon splashing along the shore and then making castles in the sand.

"What a glorious sight," sighed Tilly. "Those two certainly enjoy themselves. Even though it's been extra work, you couldn't ask for better-behaved children."

Stephanie and George proudly laid out the lunch from the basket onto a checkered cloth. There were ham and lettuce sandwiches, sliced tomatoes, fresh lemonade and hot tea. Tilly's cookies were in a tin for later.

"My goodness," said the delighted Amy, "you two have certainly done a wonderful job at making lunch."

Tilly added: "I've never had such a lovely picnic."

The children insisted on cleaning up and putting things away.

They went back to the sea and were soon concentrating on making a moat for their castle. Amy and Tilly sat in the shade, watching the children and talking. A few passing clouds began to obscure the sun. It seemed like a good time to begin packing up.

"Well, I must get home anyway and make Walter's tea," said Tilly. "He wants it punctual at four-thirty."

The children dried off and all the lunch things were put back in the car. They dropped Tilly at her house and drove back up the lane to Bower House.

After a late tea, Amy told them that they both needed a good hot bath and a hair wash, so that their parents would find them looking clean and shiny. "In the morning, we'll pack up your suitcases," said Amy. "Tilly washed and ironed your clothes yesterday, so they're well taken care of for you."

Both Amy and the children went to bed early, feeling quite sleepy after a day spent out of doors.

Right after breakfast on Saturday morning, the children packed their bags under Amy's supervision; and of course, some little containers had to be found to hold their souvenir shells. They wanted to go for a last walk in the forest and to say goodbye to the twins.

Tilly made their favourite lunch and baked some cakes for tea. "When will we see the young ones again, Miss Amy?" she enquired.

"I don't know, Tilly. Perhaps Barbara might tell me their summer plans this afternoon."

At about two o'clock, the shiny car with the children's parents arrived and they were greeted with hugs and kisses by Stephanie and George who had been waiting on the bench outside.

"Darlings!" cried Barbara. "We've missed you so much. We really must take you to Paris on a holiday next summer. We had such a wonderful time. You both look so tanned and healthy and I'm sure you've grown!"

Jeffery and Barbara both embarrassed Amy by saying many thank yous for taking care of the children.

Amy led everyone into the house as George talked to his father about the tennis games and the fun they had playing with Mrs. Bromfield's children. Stephanie started to tell them all about the hilarious luncheon at the Bromfield's. By the time she was finished, they were all laughing until they cried. George then described in detail their picnics by the sea.

Amy told everyone to catch their breath while she and Barbara got tea and cakes ready. Barbara exclaimed again on what a wonderful time the children must have had, and hoped that Amy and Tilly were not completely worn out.

As they went back to the living room, Stephanie and George came forward with two beautifully wrapped parcels.

"Mother bought these for you, Grandmother," said Stephanie with a smile.

"You certainly did a marvellous job of minding the children, Amy," said Jeffery. "Barbara and I managed to enjoy a lovely vacation in spite of my business every day."

The first parcel was a box containing a most beautiful Hermés scarf done in many shades of blue and bordered in black.

"Oh, how lovely!" said Amy. "It looks like a stained-glass window. Thank you."

The second box contained a very expensive black leather purse, shaped like a large envelope, with a chain strap.

"Thank you again," exclaimed Amy, "but I certainly didn't expect anything like this for taking care of these very good children. I'm sure these are both very expensive gifts."

"Mother, you know how lovely you'll look with these. The scarf will bring out your blue eyes," said Barbara. "These are just small tokens of our gratitude."

"Nonsense," said Amy, "but I can't help but love them. I haven't bought anything new since … ," and her voice trailed off as Barbara came over and gave her a comforting embrace.

"Now let's have our tea before it gets cold," said Amy in a shaky voice. "Stephanie, will you pass the cakes please?"

The next hour passed quickly as Barbara and Jeffery told more about their trip, and the children also told about the fair.

Soon it was time for them to leave. Jeffery put the children's bags in the car and with a few more kisses and hugs, they said goodbye and drove away.

I hope the children's parents don't notice the scars from their scrapes, Amy thought as she sighed with both relief and happiness.

She took a light snack and her favourite book upstairs to bed with her, and was soon fast asleep.

5

The following morning, Amy went off to Sunday service at St. Boniface and greeted the Vicar at the door.

"Have your young visitors gone home, Mrs. Somerset?" he asked.

"Yes, Vicar," she replied. "They were picked up by their parents yesterday. We had a wonderful two weeks together."

After service, her friend Vivian caught up with Amy and asked her to come for lunch on Wednesday and to stay for some bridge. Amy enjoyed this, so she said thank you and that she would look forward to it.

On arriving home from church, Amy had a light lunch and puttered in the garden, noticing that most of the seeds that Walter had put in had turned into neat rows of plants. She gave them a light spray of water and then sat on a deck chair on the patio and read. That evening she went to bed early again, telling herself that she must indeed be getting old to be tired out so easily.

Tilly came the next morning and soon had the house put

to rights again. She sang a medley of her favourite hymns in a happy, loud voice, a sure sign she was busy, yet enjoying herself.

The telephone in the front hall rang and, as Amy answered it, a familiar voice rang out: "Dearest, how are you? I heard that you had the grandchildren for two weeks and wondered how you survived. We haven't seen you in ages and we're wondering if you could come to town for a week's visit starting this Saturday?"

Amy had gone to school with Georgina Melville and also saw her and her husband, Basil, socially when Amy and William lived in London. Amy and Georgina had been such good friends since secretarial school days.

"Please say you will, dear," pleaded Georgina. "We have some theatre tickets, and we could do some of the fun things we used to do."

"Well, I don't know, Georgina. If you're sure that Basil wouldn't mind having me underfoot."

"You know he works nine to ten hours a day and I would love to have your company."

"Well, that would be lovely," answered Amy.

"Take the nine-thirty train on Saturday and we will meet you at the station."

"I will be looking forward to it very much, dear," answered Amy. "See you then."

As she hung up the phone, she started to think as a typical woman about what she was going to wear. Tilly was all excited when she heard the news and reminded her that she now had the beautiful Hermés scarf and her new purse to take.

"I'll help you go through your closet and see what needs to be freshened up."

"I think you're more excited than I am," joked Amy, "but it

will be fun. Georgina and I always had a good time together, even in school. I was her bridesmaid and she was mine. I do have some nice pearls and earrings and I did inherit a lovely diamond pendant and earrings from my mother. I wish I had some new pumps, but I shall get the old ones re-heeled and shined and they will look like new," said Amy. "I wonder if I should go after all?"

"Nonsense," said Tilly. "You haven't been to London since your visit to Barbara and the family at Easter. It will do you good. Now stop fussing and come and have your lunch."

After lunch, Amy went upstairs and looked through her wardrobe. Thank goodness she only bought good classic items. She selected a navy suit and a light blue summer frock and held them up to herself.

Well, I guess I haven't gained any weight, so they will fit, she said to herself, and I do have two lovely dresses for dinners and the theatre. Those gifts from Barbara will come in handy too. No one will know how penny-pinched I really am. Perhaps I will even get my hair done at my favourite salon where Georgina and I used to go.

The rest of the week passed quietly. Amy enjoyed the luncheon and bridge on Wednesday and the chance to have a good chat with her friends. She used to play every week before William took seriously ill and had told Vivian she would come back anytime she needed a fourth.

Soon it was Saturday morning and time to leave. Walter had offered to take her to the station in his car. Tilly wished her a pleasant trip, telling her not to worry about anything but having a good time.

The train left punctually and she was off to London.

Georgina and Basil were waiting on the platform, so Amy did not have to go looking for them.

"Here, hand me those bags, Amy," said Basil as he kissed her in welcome. Dark-haired Georgina kissed her too and held her in a tight and welcoming embrace.

"Amy dear, it's been ages. We are certainly looking forward to this coming week. We have so much news to catch up on," smiled Georgina. "How was the train ride? Thank goodness it isn't too long. You do look a bit tired, though. Did the children wear you out? We are going to spoil you thoroughly, aren't we Basil? We have some delightful plans, but not too many, and you will have a nice sleep-in each morning."

I wonder just how bad I look, thought Amy.

Georgina had always chattered on, hardly giving one a chance to say anything at all. Amy felt smothered in kindness already.

At their house, which faced a quiet park, Amy was shown to a lovely guestroom over-looking the garden. There were sweet-smelling pink roses on her bedside table, and the delicate white curtains fluttered in the breeze. A few magazines and a book sat on a table beside an easy chair draped with an afghan. Everything looked so comfortable.

"I'll give you about fifteen minutes to wash up and hang up your clothes and then we can have some sherry before lunch," said Georgina, as she closed the door.

Amy quickly put away her dresses in the closet, tidied her hair and washed up. Such luxury, she said to herself. This guestroom is fit for royalty.

As she looked in the mirror at her blonde hair with the grey wings on the side, her blue eyes sparkled back at her. I'm going to make myself be happy and enjoy all this, she said under her breath. This is a long overdue vacation.

Downstairs in the living room, the patio doors were open and a warm breeze stirred the curtains.

"How about a glass of sherry to revive you before lunch?" asked Basil.

"That would be lovely, thank you," Amy replied.

They chatted for a few minutes before lunch was served, everyone sipping their sherry. They went into the dining room shortly and a generous salad was served along with sole and green beans. For dessert, they had lemon syllabub and coffee. Amy felt a bit woolly-headed from the sherry so she had an extra cup of coffee to straighten herself out.

"We have tickets for a delightful musical comedy tonight at seven o'clock and if you feel up to it, dinner at this wonderful little restaurant around the corner afterwards. Would you enjoy that or are you too tired?" asked Georgina.

"Oh, you know how I love the theatre and I would look forward to it," answered Amy, smiling.

"Would you like to have some quiet for a while? I've put a brand new book in your room—very funny, and some magazines," said Georgina. "Basil has some papers to go over this afternoon and we will have a generous tea around four."

"Yes, I would welcome a little rest this afternoon," confessed Amy. "That sounds very tempting."

"Are there any special things you would like to do this week, Amy?"

"Well, I would really love to get my hair cut and styled at our old favourite salon."

"Your hair has such a lovely curl to it. I'll call this afternoon and see if we can arrange some appointments. I remember that Giorgio was always your favourite, even though he is rather temperamental," laughed Georgina.

She took Amy upstairs and asked her if there was anything else she needed.

Amy replied: "Now stop fussing, dear. I will be fine. Thank you for that lovely lunch and for inviting me to stay with you."

Amy closed her door and put on her dressing gown. She looked at a magazine and read about fifteen pages of her book before falling asleep. She was awakened by a tap at the door and with a rather unladylike snort, she called out: "Come in."

"Oh dear, did I wake you, Amy?" asked Georgina. Amy answered, trying to come back to reality and blinking her eyes: "I guess I must have nodded off after all. What time is it?"

"Three-thirty, dear," said Georgina. "Now there is no rush, so why don't you take a nice warm bath and put some sweet-smelling salts in."

Amy started to run the water but dropped the bottle of salts into the tub. She had to open the window for a few minutes in an attempt to let out some of the too-sweet odour.

Dear me, she thought, I won't need any perfume tonight with all this scent.

She put on her travelling suit again with a fresh blouse, combed her hair and freshened her face. She left the window open just a little too. The clock in the hall was chiming four as she came downstairs. Georgina and Basil were there in the living room with the tea tray set out.

Basil said: "I hear you had a nice rest this afternoon; we were hoping you would. Now, you'll enjoy the evening more."

Basil was a tall, balding man, very distinguished-looking and with a voice of authority. He was a barrister and worked as a partner at the same firm where William had worked. He did much of the courtroom work.

Tea was indeed generous with several thin sandwiches and teacakes. They were all soon full. Amy talked about the grandchildren's visit, and she entertained them with some of the hilarious events that had happened. She told them about the church fair and her favourite story about Napoleon's visit to the tea party.

"Oh, you certainly were busy, Amy, but I can understand how your life became very enjoyable," laughed Georgina. "I think two weeks was long enough, though."

"Well, I do love my grandchildren," said Amy, "they are very special to me."

"Would you like a drink before we go, Amy," asked Basil.

"No thank you, Basil. I'm afraid that the sherry before lunch went right to my head."

"Well, perhaps, we should go up and change and be ready to go by six-fifteen, then," suggested Georgina.

"You and Basil go ahead and have something to drink if you like. I'll see you down here a little after six."

Amy went up to her room and chose her gold silk print dress and pearls. My gold sandals aren't too bad, she thought.

Her dress slipped on easily and, as she looked in the full-length glass, she blinked back tears, remembering that the last time she had worn this outfit, she had gone to the theatre with William. With a last pat of her hair, she picked up her beaded satin handbag and proceeded downstairs.

"Basil has called for a taxi since it's impossible to park near the theatre," said Georgina. "Oh, Amy, you look just stunning."

"And your pink silk suit is so complimentary to your lovely complexion," Amy replied with real admiration.

"Now I'm the one that should be handing out all the compliments, ladies, so all I can do is agree that you both look smashing," laughed Basil. "I see that the taxi is just arriving. Each of you give me an arm and I'll escort you to our chariot."

Georgina and Amy laughed excitedly as the three proceeded

down the front steps to the waiting cab. It took about fifteen minutes driving through the heavy London traffic to arrive. As they did, Basil's face took on a peculiar look.

"Oh dear, oh dear. I changed jackets at the last minute and have forgotten the theatre tickets in my other pocket."

"Oh, Basil, how could you forget them?" cried Georgina.

"Well, you two ladies go along in and speak to Mr. Fitzgibbons, the manager, and tell him what happened. We are regulars and always sit in the same box, so perhaps he'll let you go to our seats. I'll be back as soon as possible."

"Well, let's do as Basil says and maybe things will work out," said Amy, trying to smooth her friend's rattled feelings.

They found Mr. Fitzgibbons greeting several of the theatregoers as they came in. Georgina spotted a tall, red-haired, but greying gentleman with him.

"Oh, it's James Carstairs. You remember the senior partner in the firm," said Georgina.

As they came up the stairs, both men turned with wide smiles on their faces, Mr. Fitzgibbons not quite recognizing Georgina, but James Carstairs greeting them both as old friends, which indeed they were.

Georgina explained their problem to Mr. Fitzgibbons, who did not seem wholly convinced until Mr. Carstairs said: "Now let me take these two little birds under my wings. Believe me, they are telling the truth. I will be happy to escort them to their box with your permission."

"Oh thank you," said Georgina quite relieved. "Basil will soon return with the tickets."

Mr. Carstairs talked to them both for a few minutes, asking after Amy's health and how she was getting along in the country. He withdrew to his own box just before the music began.

Basil appeared at the beginning of the play much harassed

and drew glaring looks for the disturbance he caused. He kept very quiet after that until he finally started to relax and enjoy the play, laughing heartily several times. Georgina and Amy were highly amused too and also enjoyed the catchy tunes.

After the long first act, everyone decided to get up and stretch their legs for a moment. Basil half hid near the curtains in case any of his clients had seen him come in late.

"Darling, how did you manage to get back in such record time?" asked Georgina.

"I promised the driver a large tip for speed, so he took some back streets. I really must apologize. I have never forgotten the theatre tickets before."

In a few minutes, they returned to their box and enjoyed the rest of the performance just as much as the first.

It was only a short walk around the corner to Antony's Restaurant, a very elegant place. Since Basil had made reservations and knew the proprietor, they were soon ensconced in a plush booth in a corner. They were each handed an embellished menu with a flourish, and Basil asked the ladies if they would mind if he ordered some champagne to celebrate Amy's arrival.

Amy said: "Oh no," and Georgina said: "Oh yes" at the same time.

"You are so extravagant, my dear Basil," laughed Amy as the champagne arrived within minutes in a silver bucket.

"Actually, this is a double celebration. I had success in a court case yesterday too, so I'm really in that kind of mood."

They toasted each other when their glasses had been filled and started to look at the menu. Antony himself came over and announced three specials for the evening.

After much looking and talking, it seemed funny that they all ordered the special salad and the filet done with a béarnaise sauce.

"Now Basil dear, you usually go for something totally outlandish," exclaimed Georgina.

"Well, it seemed just the thing that would hit the spot tonight, dear."

At that moment, James Carstairs and another man passed their table. He stopped to say hello and introduced his friend, another lawyer of course, and an old school fellow. Basil took this opportunity to thank James for his assistance.

"Did you enjoy the show everyone?" he asked.

They all nodded and agreed with enthusiasm "Oh yes!" and "Certainly did!"

"Are you going to the Legal Society Dinner on Wednesday night, Basil?" Mr. Carstairs asked.

"Yes indeed, and I am bringing these two beautiful ladies along."

"Well, we will see you on Wednesday, then," Mr. Carstairs nodded. "I am glad you are coming too, Mrs. Somerset. Good evening everyone."

"I forgot to tell you about that," laughed Georgina. "While you were resting, I also made hair appointments on Wednesday morning at ten o'clock for both of us with Giorgio. He will do your hair first and then mine."

They took a leisurely two hours to eat their wonderful dinner, and then hailed a taxi to take them home.

Since they had been up so late, they decided to go to eleven o'clock service on Sunday. The boys' choir was certainly an inspiration. Lady Brocklehurst, Georgina's grandmother and also an old friend of Amy's grandmother, had more or less ordered them to come to lunch at two o'clock on Sunday afternoon.

"I hope you don't mind, dear Amy," Georgina had told her yesterday, "but you know what an old tartar she is. I couldn't say no."

Amy had agreed, having had a few run-ins with Lady Brocklehurst herself. It was she who had spurred the girls to take up secretarial work in their late teens and had even found them jobs in the same office where the original Mr. Carstairs was a founder.

"You modern misses must be independent and work for your living nowadays. No idle hands you know," she had drummed into them.

It was a happy coincidence that they had both married lawyers in the firm and that they had stayed such long-time friends. They made sure to arrive promptly at two and Denby, the butler, ushered them in.

"Come in, come in," said Lady Brocklehurst in a brisk voice. "Let me take a look at you." They all did as commanded.

"Well I must say you're all looking well; a little older perhaps," she observed. "I plan to live to be a hundred," she said with sharp sparkling eyes. "I will be ninety-eight next week, and proud of it."

"You look well too, Grandmother," said Georgina, with a straight face. "How are you feeling?"

"Don't toady to me, young lady," snapped Lady Brocklehurst.

She had a softer tone for Amy, remembering how painful it was to lose a husband as she had lost her own ten years ago. A few gentle questions about Amy's daughter and grandchildren seemed to satisfy her curiosity.

"How about you, Basil—still setting the world on fire with

your trials? Though I must admit that you are a very capable young man."

The butler announced that lunch was served and Basil took Lady Brocklehurst's arm, followed by the two ladies. Lunch was very delicious, having been made by her French cook. It was a wonderful chicken dish and a fruit salad with greens. A light wine was served also, with some cheeses and biscuits to follow. Of course, Lady Brocklehurst did most of the talking in a very stringent manner, but with a sense of humour thrown in now and then too.

At three-thirty, Lady Brocklehurst excused herself, saying that she must have her rest, and said goodbye graciously. They thanked her for her wonderful hospitality, and took their leave.

After a late tea, Basil went off to his library to prepare for the next day's case, and the girls chatted comfortably in front of the fireplace.

Georgina enquired on how Amy was getting along. Amy admitted that she had been feeling rather sorry for herself since William's death, but just lately she had forced herself to keep busy, and this was helping.

"My family and friends are so good to me and I found that keeping the grandchildren for two weeks, and now coming back to London to visit you, have made me feel much better. Tilly is also such a comfort to me.

"I've decided to start back into the bridge club and I just helped out with the Jumble Sale for the Ladies' Institute. I guess it's just up to me to make the effort."

Georgina replied: "You are right in all you say, Amy. I realize how difficult it must have been for you at first. Who wouldn't feel down? But now you're getting back into life and you do look so much brighter."

"Well, this has certainly been an enjoyable day, but if you don't mind, I'm ready for my bed now, Georgina. Thank you again. You are a wonderful friend."

They hugged each other and said "Good night."

6

Basil left for work before eight o'clock the next morning and Amy and Georgina ate breakfast together about nine.

"Well, what would you like to do today?" Georgina asked. "Remember our old friend from school, Dorothea Selby, now Dorothea Cox? She told me to call this morning if we felt like going out for lunch."

"I think I would enjoy that," answered Amy with a smile. "I haven't seen her since William's funeral, and everything was such a blur at the time."

"Well, let's attack Harrod's this morning and our secret dress shop this afternoon. I'll give Dorothea a call and set up a luncheon at a café in the area," said Georgina briskly. "Go and get dressed and I'll see you back downstairs in about an hour."

They both refreshed themselves and chose light and bright outfits since it was going to be a warm day. Amy wore her pretty blue summer frock.

"You certainly have kept your figure well," commented Georgina.

"I guess I'll have to be a little careful with all these dinners and lunches," Amy replied with a laugh.

Since they weren't meeting Dorothea until one o'clock, they went directly to Harrod's but were soon separated in a large crowd at a food-making demonstration. They both went around the outskirts of the crowd each looking for the other. Suddenly, they literally bumped into one another behind a post. They laughed aloud but were told to "hush" so that the chef could be heard.

They went to the make-up counter and tried on different coloured lipsticks with the guidance of a haughty clerk and finally each decided on a flattering shade. They then strolled about the women's clothing section until near lunchtime.

"I always find it so confusing facing all this merchandise, don't you Amy?" asked Georgina.

The café was not far, so they decided to walk. As Georgina was talking to the hostess, Dorothea arrived.

"Hello, my dears," she said with a smile. "I'm so happy to see you. We have so much news to catch up on." She hugged them both.

The hostess led them to a booth and handed each a menu.

"Now I'm only having a salad and tea for lunch," laughed Amy. "Georgina seems to be on a campaign to fatten me up."

Since she was setting such a good example, the other two couldn't help but do the same. There was much laughter and "remember when" during lunch, while they also caught up on current events.

About two-thirty, they parted company and Amy and Georgina headed for their favourite dress store, Madame Zolie's. The proprietress greeted them warmly, especially Amy whom she had not seen in some time.

They tried on a few things and Amy was very tempted by a

rose-coloured suit, but remembered her tight budget and said: "Not now. I really would have no occasion to wear it in Ferndene. It is a little dressy."

Georgina looked at her with a puzzled frown and decided that she would only take the green blouse that she had chosen. She refrained from making any comment to Amy, but several thoughts were in the back of her mind. By this time, it was getting late, so they took a taxi home.

They both decided to have a rest before dinner as Basil had called saying he wouldn't be home until six. Amy said she would meet them both downstairs at six-thirty. She retired to the beautiful guest room and laid down for a brief rest before changing for dinner. Feeling much refreshed, she was able to greet everyone with a sunny smile.

Georgina's cook had made another delicious meal, which they all appreciated. After dinner, they talked in the living room for a while and everyone went up to bed at an early hour.

Tuesday was usually Georgina's bridge day and she asked Amy if she would mind substituting for one of the ladies. Lunch and bridge were being held at Joan Ridgeway's house a few blocks away.

"That would be lovely," replied Amy. "You know how much I enjoy bridge. I hope my game is good enough."

"Don't worry about that," laughed Georgina, "we spend most of the time talking."

Amy managed to hold her own that day. In fact, she ended up tops in score. Everyone accused her of being too shy about her prowess, which made her smile. She credited her success to good luck.

To show her appreciation for Georgina's hospitality, Amy bought her a lovely bouquet of flowers, under much protest of course. The flowers looked beautiful on the hall table.

Basil came home from the office at about six and after he had a chance to change, they had a delightful dinner of roast lamb with mixed vegetables on the side.

Again Basil excused himself saying that he needed an hour to look over some papers, so the two girls sat in the living room having a nice chat. Georgina praised Amy's bridge, but she protested again saying the cards were some of the best that she had ever seen.

Wednesday was going to be a busy day so the girls started at a leisurely pace by having their breakfast in their dressing gowns.

"We can't be late for the hairdresser's," exclaimed Georgina, suddenly noticing the time. "You know how temperamental Giorgio is. We also have to take a taxi."

They managed to be ready in plenty of time and reached the hairdresser's with twenty minutes to spare. Giorgio, a short, thin man with black hair done in a ponytail, came to get Amy first and greeted her with a kiss on each cheek.

"You look as radiant as always, my dear Mrs. Somerset. Your hair is still your crowning glory."

"We're being treated to a manicure too," called Georgina, "and Basil is footing the bill. We must do him credit tonight at the dinner."

Soon Giorgio was snipping here and there, with Amy worrying about what the outcome would be. The girl who had washed her hair looked very emaciated and had an earring in her nose. I hope she doesn't get colds very often, Amy giggled to herself.

"There you are, my dear," exclaimed Giorgio with a satisfied look on his face. He showed her all around her head with a mirror. "Your waves and curls make it so easy to do your hair. I will go over again how you can do it yourself until next time. Maybe then we could make these silver wings on the sides golden," he joked.

"Thank you," said Amy. "I am very pleased. Only you have that magic touch."

"Now you two beautiful ladies change places. I am such a fortunate man to have a chance to create my work on two lovely tresses."

Amy sat quietly while her manicure was done, meanwhile glancing in the mirror to see who that well-coiffed person could be. He certainly is a master, she thought. How much better I look and feel.

Giorgio had shaped Georgina's lovely dark brown hair and shortened it a little, so that she looked much younger.

"Well, at least we can recognize each other," laughed Georgina as they left the salon and complimented each other on their hair.

Amy said she would have to thank Basil for the manicure treat, adding that she hadn't had one in a very long time. Georgina quickly changed the subject and suggested a nice salad and tea lunch at a place around the corner.

Over lunch, they discussed what to wear that evening. Amy decided on her beautiful new Hermés scarf with her dark blue dress and blue bag.

They took a taxi home and relaxed on the terrace, reading the newspaper and some current magazines so as not to disturb their hair and nails. Basil called to say that he would be late again, so they went ahead with their tea at about four.

Amy took her time with a leisurely bath and dressed carefully, admiring the beautiful scarf as she tied it two or three different ways before settling on the most attractive outcome.

She was downstairs shortly after six, as they were again going by taxi to the dinner. Georgina looked lovely in a moss-green dress that matched her eyes, and Basil looked very handsome in his tuxedo and bow tie.

"Thank you for the manicure today, Basil. It was a wonderful treat," commented Amy.

As they arrived at the club, Amy was a little nervous wondering if she would know enough people.

"Stay with me, darling," said Georgina in a comforting whisper. "You'll be surprised. First of all, everyone will be here from the firm and you know them and all their wives. You know of course that Mr. Carstairs is still a bachelor."

Amy did enjoy the brief half-hour before dinner and reacquainted herself with the people from the firm. It was difficult in a way since she and her husband had socialized with these couples in the past, but they were all very kind and many people came up to talk to her.

As dinner was called, she found herself placed between Basil and James Carstairs. Georgina was between Basil and Nigel Fleming, another solicitor.

"Well, my dear Mrs. Somerset, how are you enjoying your visit?" asked Mr. Carstairs. "You are radiant tonight and look much rested," he said kindly.

Amy, with a laugh, said: "Basil and Georgina are spoiling me dreadfully, but it is a nice change and I enjoy being in London again."

The conversation at the table was easy and friendly and Amy

felt completely relaxed. Halfway through the fish course, Amy's serviette slipped to the floor. Mr. Carstairs, with a slight smile, picked it up and said: "I believe this is yours." Much flustered, Amy tried to answer gracefully and put it back on her lap.

In the middle of dessert, her satin handbag slipped from her lap. She bent to retrieve it and banged heads with Mr. Carstairs who laughed and with a little mischief in his voice said: "If you will call me James, I will give it back."

Amy smiled and answered: "You must think me a clumsy woman—James. Thank you."

There was a short speech from the president of the Law Society and everyone went into the ballroom to dance. Georgina and Amy were both asked to dance, and then James Carstairs approached Amy and invited her to sit near the windows with him so they could have a chance to chat.

"Not that your dancing is bad, but I am afraid that mine is, and I have something in particular to say to you," he stated.

Amy, rather bewildered, replied: "Certainly, er—James, I would welcome a little rest."

As they sat down, he hesitated and then said: "I'm not sure where to begin, but being a solicitor I will just be forthright. My secretary, Doris, is getting married soon and I must find a suitable replacement for her. I know that this may seem sudden and presumptuous, but I know what a wonderful job you did for William, and well, I just have to ask whether you could be interested in coming back to work at the office?"

Amy was quite taken aback, but James pressed on: "I feel confident that your skills would be up to the standards required. Your computer skills may cause you to hesitate, but let me assure you that the practice of law is still mainly about clarity and accuracy—that will never change.

"We do more on the computer now, but we employ a consultant who has developed an extensive library of precedents, so that whole documents can be created by simply recalling work that has been done before, and stored for just that purpose. The most important skills are your shorthand and your command of the language. The rest can be quickly learned, and help is always close at hand."

He waited for Amy to respond. She was dumbfounded and it must have shown on her face. Finally, she was able to say: "It certainly is a sudden idea; I will need time to think about it."

He said: "I am sorry to spring this on you so suddenly, and in these circumstances, but time is closing in on me. Might I ask you to think about it and to give me an indication of your interest in a week or so?"

"There's no need to apologize," said Amy. "I'm flattered by the offer and will try to get back to you early next week."

"I'm grateful to you, and I should add that if you accept, Doris's flat may be available for lease as she and her husband will be moving to Glasgow. The flat is quite handy to the office.

"You wouldn't need to start for two or three weeks, so that would give you time to settle a few things. I would try not to be too much of a taskmaster, and the work is pretty well the same kind of law that William practised. You were so efficient and capable."

"Well, as I said before, this is all so sudden. I'll need to think it over, but I will try to call you on Monday," she answered with a tremulous smile.

"I hope I haven't upset you. I certainly didn't mean to. I am very set in my ways after all these years, and would much rather have an experienced secretary during my last two years of work. I plan to retire then, you know," he informed her. "A little bit of travel sounds good to me after all the many hours that this business entails."

Basil came over at that moment and asked Amy to dance with him again. He was a marvellous dancer; Georgina had told her before that it was one of his best talents. Soon, it was time to go home, since all the men had to be up early for work the next day.

"I had a lovely time," Amy said to Basil and Georgina. "Thank you for including me."

"And you didn't feel the least bit awkward, did you darling?" responded Georgina.

"Except for a couple of faux pas," laughed Amy, as she told them about dropping first her serviette and then her purse.

Understandably, Amy had difficulty in falling asleep that night. She had many thoughts running through her mind: Can I still do this?—Is two years more than I can take?—Could I find someone to lease my house?—What about Tilly?—What will Barbara say?

She made a mental list of the positives and negatives of accepting this job offer. The positives were clearly more convincing—she needed the money; the offer was quite flattering; the work would be familiar to her; and she would enjoy living in London again on a short-term basis.

As she fell off to sleep, she finally admitted to herself: This must be done to save Bower House.

The next morning, after a late breakfast, Amy decided to tell Georgina about the proposed job with Mr. Carstairs. Georgina was very concerned when Amy confessed that she was finding it difficult to pay the bills.

"Darling, I had no idea you were under such pressure," she exclaimed.

Amy explained that if she could work for two years and lease out her house at a favourable rental, she could acquire a wonderful nest egg that would make her quite comfortable. She had pretty well made her decision and felt quite sure about it.

"Perhaps you should consult Barbara and Jeffery and see what they have to say."

"I must admit that their reaction has been my main concern. I'll give Barbara a call right now and invite myself for dinner tonight or tomorrow night."

"Well, you might as well settle it as soon as possible rather than disturb yourself any longer," agreed Georgina.

Barbara, recognizing Amy's anxiety on the phone, invited her mother to come over that very night, as Jeffery was free too. They had dinner at six, a little early, but they wanted to have a couple of hours to discuss Amy's dilemma.

Since Amy herself had decided to accept the job as a good way to settle her problems, she really just wanted Barbara and Jeffery's approval. They were both sympathetic to her situation and offered as an alternative that she move in with them or allow them to give her an allowance. She said firmly: "Thank you, my dears; you are loving and generous, but I do enjoy my independence and I really think this will be a good step for me. I admit I've been moping a bit since your father's death and this may stir me out of the doldrums while giving me a secure nest egg. I can't bear the thought of selling Bower House but I'm sure that I could lease it with a very good return. A reputable tenant must be found of course, but the real estate agent can work that out for me."

"Oh Mother, you seem to have it all planned out already. Are you sure you want to do this? It may be too much for you," exclaimed Barbara in a worried tone.

"Yes, my decision is made. I'll try to see the other secretary's flat before I leave London. I understand that it's in a genteel neighbourhood, and just a short bus ride from the office."

"You're a brave woman, Amy. This is a bold step," said Jeffery, giving her a kiss on the forehead. "Now let me give you a ride back to Georgina's. It has just started to rain."

On Friday morning, Amy said to Georgina: "Since my train isn't going until after two tomorrow, I'm going to call Doris, the secretary, and see if I can view the flat in the morning." The matter was easily arranged and Georgina offered to come too.

Amy's last evening in London featured another wonderful play, and dinner at a different restaurant.

James Carstairs waved to Amy as he sat in his box near them at the theatre.

"I'm not really checking up on you, my dear Mrs. Somerset," he said with a laugh when he saw them on the way out. "I look forward to hearing from you next week. Good evening everyone."

On Saturday morning, Georgina and Amy went to see Doris's flat and were greeted enthusiastically.

"I won't say a word to anyone, Mrs. Somerset," she said. "Mr. Carstairs told me about his conversation with you and I'm sure he'll be very pleased to have you as his secretary. I'm getting married three weeks from today, but I'll be off the week before to finalize arrangements. My husband-to-be and I are going away on our honeymoon, and I believe you know we're then moving to Glasgow."

She showed the ladies around the apartment, which was very neat. It had its own bathroom, a small kitchen and a large window overlooking the garden.

"Mrs. Fillmore is a wonderful landlady. She and her husband live downstairs and we have a cup of tea together now and then," said Doris. "The flat comes furnished except for my personal mementoes. The fireplace works nicely too and I enjoy it on cold nights."

Amy was mentally picturing some of her own things strewn about, perhaps some cushions and pictures and little mementoes of her own. Yes, I could be very happy here, she told herself.

"I promised to call Mr. Carstairs early next week, Doris, so I will call you also to tell you what has been settled."

The rent was mentioned and seemed just fine to Amy. She knew approximately what private secretaries earned and the rent seemed to fit within her budget.

"Thank you so much, Doris. I'll probably make my calls on Monday."

"Well, things seem to be falling into place," she said to Georgina.

"It does seem like fate somehow," answered Georgina.

They went back home to lunch with Basil, who said that he was happy to hear how things had worked out for Amy.

After many thank yous, a few tearful goodbyes and a promise to call them on Monday too, Amy was on board the train and on her way back to Ferndene.

7

Walter was at the station to meet Amy when she arrived, and he commented on how relaxed she looked.

"Your visit seems to have done you a lot of good, Mrs. Somerset," he said, pushing his cap up on his brow. At home, Tilly was waiting, everything clean and shining, and a beautiful vase of fresh roses adorned the hall table.

"You look so happy my dear," said Tilly. "Did you have a good time?"

"Oh yes! I had a wonderful visit and was treated like royalty. After I get straightened up and my clothes put away, could you stay and have a cup of tea with me and a little chat, Tilly?"

"Of course. Take your time while I get the tea things ready. I have made some fresh cakes for you too."

Over tea and some tears on both sides, Amy explained what had happened and what she had decided to do.

"I must keep Bower House somehow, Tilly. It has been my anchor and refuge through most of my life."

Tilly was very understanding and said that she suspected

something was amiss, especially when Walter was asked to enlarge the vegetable garden.

"Have you noticed how well the plants have come along?" she asked. They went out together to look at the neat rows of new growth. "The house has been scrubbed from top to bottom while you were gone, so we can decide on Monday what else there is to do."

After Sunday service, Amy asked her friend Vivian Langford over for afternoon tea, as she wanted to talk to her about something important. When Amy explained her plans, Vivian was very surprised at first, but agreed that Amy had made a wise and brave choice. She promised to help in any way that she could.

Amy squared her shoulders after breakfast on Monday morning and dialed James Carstairs. Doris put her through immediately and he came on the line, saying in an anxious voice: "Hello, Mrs. Somerset. You are certainly true to your word. Have you made a decision?"

"Since we last spoke, I've given the matter much thought and spoken to my daughter and my closest friends, and I'm pleased to reply that I will gladly accept the job. I can start in two weeks, which seems to fit in with Doris's plans. I'll come in the week before on Thursday and Friday to spend some time with her. I'll need to know her routines in order to make the transition as painless as possible for both you and me."

"I'm so pleased by your decision, and grateful too, Mrs. Somerset," Mr. Carstairs replied with emotion. "Have you had a chance to speak to Doris or her landlord yet about her apartment?"

"I'm very interested in taking over her lease," Amy replied, "and I hope to finalize arrangements shortly."

"By the way, since you'll be living in London, would you have any interest in obtaining a tenant for your house?"

"As a matter of fact, I would be willing to lease it," Amy replied.

"In that case, I would like to propose it to a great old school chum of mine, Sir John Beaton, and his wife, Lady Jane, who might be interested in leasing. He's been in the diplomatic corps and they've been looking for a comfortable place outside of London. May I allow them to call you tomorrow? Don't be afraid to ask a good rent. They can surely afford it," he said with a chuckle.

"I certainly would welcome their call, especially if you know them and recommend them. Thank you very much for your generosity. I want to assure you that you can depend on me entirely."

"I know I can, Mrs. Somerset. That is why I know you'll make an excellent secretary. Goodbye for now, and thank you again."

Amy called Doris and finalized plans to meet her again at her apartment.

Amy kept Tilly up to date on her plans. Tilly was quite excited to hear about the Beatons and felt that they certainly would want the house.

"Do you remember my niece Elsie who lives in town?" she asked Amy. "She worked in the catering business in London for a few years and very fancy things they did. If ever your tenants wanted to have some guests for dinner or a party, I'm sure she would love the occasional work. No doubt they have some very elegant friends."

The next day, Sir John Beaton called Amy to say that he had

talked to his old friend, Carstairs. Amy's house seemed to be just the sort of home that they were looking for and he asked if there was any chance of coming the following day to see it. Amy took a deep breath and in a composed voice invited them to tea at about two–thirty.

"That would be splendid, if we are not putting you out," he replied.

"Oh no," Amy said, hoping that Tilly could be there to help serve. "I'll be happy to meet you."

Tilly was all excited again, planning something nice for tea and saying to Amy: "Do you think they'll keep me on? Perhaps they have their own help."

"We'll see tomorrow," replied Amy, trying at the same time to think of which flowers were left in the garden that she could bring in the house.

Thank goodness the sun was shining brightly the next day. She and Tilly aired out the house and Amy picked some lovely bouquets. The roses and clematis were at their best too and everything looked very welcoming.

Sir John and Lady Jane Beaton were right on time and greeted Amy with smiles and how-do-you-dos. The walkway leading up to the house looked inviting and Lady Jane commented on what a beautiful bower the flowers made.

"I notice that your home is called Bower House. How appropriate," commented Lady Jane. "A lovely name for a lovely home."

Amy invited them in and showed them slowly around the house. They seemed to think it charming and were taken with the terrace garden.

Tea was served and Tilly was introduced to them. When she was out of earshot, they asked Amy if she thought that Tilly would ever consider staying on as part-time help. Amy encouraged them to ask her directly.

"Yes, I would," Tilly answered. "Usually, I come over every morning at seven-thirty and stay until one-thirty, except Sundays. Would that be acceptable? Also, I have a niece who was in the catering business, who would be available to help cook and serve if you wished to entertain for dinner."

Conversation flowed easily over tea, Lady Jane saying she had known Amy's grandmother and what a grande dame she had been. Amy mentioned that her grandparents had bought and furnished this house many years ago.

She decided to leave them for a moment to give them a chance to talk things over. When she came back, the Beatons were beaming and nodding in agreement.

"We would love to lease your home, my dear Mrs. Somerset. We are thinking of a two-year lease. James Carstairs mentioned a figure to us that seems very reasonable for the rental of such a charming place. It is furnished in such good taste."

Amy blinked her eyes at the figure mentioned but was wise enough not to say anything. She suggested that they speak again to Tilly to confirm that she was committed to stay on. Tilly was more than agreeable, especially when they stated that they would be happy to pay extra for any additional duties.

Sir Beaton handed Amy a cheque for the first month's rent. Lady Beaton interjected that she preferred to bring her own linens.

I wonder if they are monogrammed, thought Amy with a smile.

A date was set for their moving in, and they left with much good will on both sides.

Amy and Tilly talked for at least half an hour after that over another cup of tea. Tilly said: "They seem very nice and not too full of themselves at all, more like kindly older people. I think I'll enjoy working for them."

Amy then called Barbara. Barbara insisted on helping her mother move in to her new flat on the weekend before her job started.

"Come and stay at our place while you go to the office and find your way with Doris," she added.

"You're so thoughtful, my dear," Amy said with a catch in her voice. "I'll talk to you again soon."

Of course, she had to let Georgina know what had happened. She also called her friend Vivian, who was overjoyed at the way things were working out. Then finally, she called Mr. Carstairs to thank him for sending the Beatons to her, and she gave him a slight scold for the rather large rental fee he had recommended.

"I'm glad everything worked out, Mrs. Somerset. You know that this was all done for purely selfish reasons."

Doris was very happy to learn that her flat would be occupied, and added that a woman came one day a week to clean.

After a light dinner, Amy was so drained from all the excitement, she retired early, not even reading a half a dozen pages before she was sound asleep.

The next several days passed quickly as she prepared for her big move. Amy met Mrs. Epsom-Smythe at the grocer's. She was greeted with the usual loud booming voice: "What's this I hear about you moving to London? Of course, we will all miss you, especially our Women's Institute. At least, you had the good sense to lease your house to quality tenants who will add tone to our village." She added with a sniff: "Perhaps, we can get Lady

Beaton to join the Institute. I shall ask her personally. Well perhaps you will be back for a visit now and then. We will indeed miss you," she said with feeling. "Goodbye and good luck to you."

"Thank you, Mrs. Epsom-Smythe. I'm sure that I'll be visiting frequently. I have many good friends here and I want to keep in touch since I'll be returning after my two-year work term."

Amy had dinner one evening at Vivian and Jim Langford's and was given their best wishes and an open-ended invitation to return for a visit to Ferndene at any time.

Jane Barnaby and her husband Ian invited her for tea on Saturday. The twins were on their best behaviour, dressed alike in blue cotton outfits. They sat at their little nursery table in the corner using the little china set which was brought out only on special occasions. The grown-ups had a chance for a pleasant visit and, at the end, Tommy and Trudy presented Amy with coloured pictures with their names printed on the bottom.

"You're always such good children and thank you very much for the lovely pictures," said Amy with feeling. She also thanked Jane and Ian for the delightful tea and went on her way.

Mrs. Bromfield also invited her for tea, and Amy thanked her again for providing the tennis and swimming during the grandchildren's visit.

"Well, my children really enjoyed it too," she said with a smile. Mrs. Bromfield actually laughed over the incident with the dog Napoleon, saying: "I was very upset with my neighbour at the time, but the re-telling of the story more than makes up for the annoyance."

On Wednesday, Amy left for London. She had packed a light bag and went on the morning train. Barbara was waiting for her at the station and took her to lunch.

"Well, my dear," said Amy, "a new part of my life is beginning. I must admit I'm a bit anxious about my ability to do this job well. I feel confident about my typing skills, since I do all my correspondence on the typewriter but I've been practising my shorthand."

Barbara replied: "You always were an excellent secretary. Mr. Carstairs knows you and you are familiar with the offices and how they work. It has been only four years since you worked for father. Doris said she would spend the next two mornings helping you find your way about. On Saturday morning, Jeffery and I will take you out to Bower House to pick up your things and move them into your flat."

"Perhaps, I'll go to see my landlady today and give her the first month's rent. Do you think we might take a little time and get me some new, serviceable shoes for the office?"

In the next few days, she accomplished her goals. Doris was efficient and the office was very well organized. It appeared to be run very much like her husband's used to be.

"Mr. Carstairs misses his lunch half the time being so busy, so by one o'clock make sure you have a sandwich and tea sent up. At four, I also serve him tea and biscuits; I keep a tin here in the cupboard. I'm sure he would never think about eating if it weren't for us," she added with a proprietary air and a wink.

"My fiancé has already helped me move some things to my Mum and Dad's house, so the flat should be clean and ready for you on Saturday morning. I've left a list of some of the nearby shops for you too."

"Thank you, Doris," answered Amy. "I can see that you've been very efficient indeed, in all ways."

Saturday came, and all went smoothly. Amy had been organizing her packing for days so there were no crises. There were real tears as she said goodbye to Tilly and promised that she would call her.

When they got to London, Barbara helped her to make up her bed and to put away the linens. Amy had brought her prized afghan and some pillows that really brightened up the living room. They decided which pictures went where and what objects and favourite books looked best, and soon the flat looked like it was her own.

"Thank you, Barbara," said Amy. "I'm very pleased."

Jeffery had gone to the shops and come back with some beautiful flowers to brighten up the flat. He had also picked up some fish-and-chips that smelled positively delicious. They took a little stroll together after lunch and found a wonderful grocer's that stocked all kinds of goods including prepared foods, particularly meat pies and other ready-made baked goods. Amy did some basic shopping and Barbara and Jeffery helped her to store things away.

"Thank you, my dears," she smiled, giving them each a hug. "You're wonderful to me and I'm very fortunate to be blessed with you both. Please tell the grandchildren that I'll have them over for tea next week, but I must get myself organized first."

The next morning, she attended service at St. Alban's and met the Vicar. He was very gracious and assured her that new members were always welcome. She spent the afternoon choosing her wardrobe for her first day at work and decided to bring a lunch from home every day as an economy.

8

On Monday morning, Amy made sure that she was up at seven. She had a generous breakfast with egg, toast and tea. She dressed in a light blue suit with a print blouse and her new shoes. Barbara had insisted that she get a large handbag to match, so she felt very well dressed.

The bus went by her door every twenty minutes and it was just a twenty-minute ride to the office. She was there at eight-thirty, fifteen minutes early. James Carstairs was already busy working at his desk, and he said with a smile: "Trying to beat your boss to the office, Mrs. Somerset?"

She reddened, but managed to grin.

"Well, I wasn't sure how the bus transportation would work out."

"I'll have a couple of letters ready for dictation in about fifteen minutes." She hung up her jacket and got out the pencils and pad and organized her work station to her liking. In fifteen minutes, she went in ready for dictation, but as she sat down, she knocked over his stand of pens and pencils. Amy reddened again and apologized as she picked them up.

"Now, now, don't worry," laughed Mr. Carstairs. "Being your first day, things will not be easy."

As he dictated, she was pleasantly surprised that she was still quite good at shorthand, and that she was able to keep up. Soon the letters had been typed and they were ready for him to read and sign. She answered the phone several times, and Mr. Carstairs accepted all the calls, thanking her each time. He asked her to find three files for him, which she did promptly.

"You're coming along just fine, Mrs. Somerset," he exclaimed with a twinkle in his eye. "These letters are absolutely perfect, no mistakes. I think we'll do well together."

By one o'clock, he had not had lunch, so she buzzed him and asked what he would like.

"I had forgotten all about lunch," he said. "Perhaps, you could order me a ham-and-cheese sandwich, no mustard, and some tea." She took these in to his office on a nicely arranged tray and added a few biscuits too.

"My, my," he laughed. "I can see I'll be well taken care of. Did you eat your own lunch yet?"

She confessed she hadn't but promised to do so right away.

At four o'clock, she gave Mr. Carstairs his tea. At five, she was wondering about whether or not to go home as it was supposed to be the end of her day, when his door opened and he said: "Please go home now, Mrs. Somerset. You have done an excellent job. I'm going to finish up some papers here, and then I'll be on my way. See you tomorrow morning."

She answered good night with a smile. Amy picked up a meat pie from the grocer's on her way home. It was fresh and hot from the oven, so she just made herself a quick salad and tea for dinner. The first day was over. She was totally drained and except for spilling the pencils, had managed to get through surprisingly well.

On Wednesday, Mr. Carstairs went out for lunch and continued on to a meeting for the rest of the afternoon, but Amy had plenty of typing to do. By Friday, she was feeling very exhausted, not being used to working full time.

Of course, the grandchildren wanted to come over to see her flat, so she had the family for tea on Saturday. Afterwards, they went out for a walk together, Stephanie and George exclaiming at all the shops nearby. George spotted The Fish-and-Chips Shoppe and declared that he would have fish-and-chips every night if he lived here. Barbara had begged Amy to come for dinner on Sunday, and she could not resist.

She made friends with some of the other secretaries and occasionally had lunch with them when Mr. Carstairs was away. They weren't sure how to treat her at first since she had been a partner's wife, but as she had also worked as William's secretary, the barriers did start to fall.

Her favourite co-worker was Josie. She was no bigger than a minute, had a sunny smile with a ready laugh and a joke for everyone. She was getting married in September to a stockbroker. They had been engaged for a year. Josie told her the story of how they had met at school when they were young. He had pulled her pigtails and she had pushed him in the mud. They had not seen each other for years until they had met at a party over a year ago.

Who could help not loving the sweet girl? Her curly blonde hair shone like a halo around her head. She had glowing grey eyes and was one of the best secretaries in the firm.

A few days later, Josie's life was turned upside down—her fiancé had been killed by a taxi on the way to work. Everyone seemed to come together in sympathy for the poor girl. There was a very large attendance at the funeral. Poor Josie's head was bowed down in sorrow. She went away for a month before finally returning to her job, but the sparkle had gone from her eyes like a snuffed candle.

Josie and Amy talked almost every day at lunch time. It seemed to help ease her grief. The office staff was close, like an extended family. Amy told Josie about her own recent loss and how she had found that keeping busy was helping to ease her sorrow. Their shared grief proved to be a bond that led to a fast friendship despite their difference in age.

September third, the first Saturday of the month, was Amy's birthday. Barbara and Jeffery and the children were taking her out for dinner. Jeffery was picking her up at six and bringing her to their house. The children were very excited and after wishing her "Happy Birthday" and giving her hugs and kisses, they brought out a beautiful birthday present all done up in shiny blue ribbon. As Amy opened it she gasped, for she saw a beautiful sky-blue cashmere twin sweater set.

"Oh, my dears," she said. "This is too much!"

"Now Mother, you'll look beautiful in it, and you can wear it anywhere," Barbara said with a smile.

"Being a working woman now, you need more clothes, Grandmother," said Stephanie seriously.

Amy thanked everyone and gave them each a kiss. Soon they were off to a fancy restaurant for dinner, Stephanie looking adorable in a blue dress and George in a coat and tie. He confided to Grandmother that this was a new outfit as he had outgrown the old one.

Dinner was delicious and there was another surprise at

the end when a lovely cake with candles was brought out and placed before Amy. Her eyes sparkled with tears as she made a wish and blew out all the candles.

"Now you get your wish, Grandmother," said Stephanie, "but don't tell or it won't come true."

They all had a piece and of course George, after much pleading, was allowed a second.

"I don't know where you put it!" exclaimed his father.

The next morning they all went to the Cathedral to hear a visiting boys' choir at the service. They certainly did sound heavenly.

After a walk in the park and a lovely lunch, Amy declared that she simply must get back to her flat. Jeffery, George and Stephanie drove her back after she had thanked them all for the beautiful sweater set and the delightful weekend.

"We like having you in town, Grandmother," said Stephanie, fondly. "We all get to see you more often."

Amy went up to her flat, put away her things and decided to get some groceries. This family-run business was open from 7 A.M. until 8 P.M., seven days a week, so it was very convenient. She picked up a few necessary things and went back upstairs to put them away. She had treated herself to a lovely bouquet of sweet peas, one of her favourite flowers and they certainly looked pretty on the table.

Tilly called near teatime to chat. She asked Amy if she liked her job and her new flat. Amy answered in the affirmative and gave her a few details. She asked Tilly how she was getting along with Sir John and Lady Beaton.

"Oh, they're wonderful old dears," she cried. "I must take Lady Beaton a tray in the morning though. She has a bit of arthritis and finds it difficult to get going. Sir John now likes to go for a twenty-minute walk before breakfast to prove he's still hearty.

They seem to like my cooking, especially my scones; and High Tea was served twice," she added proudly.

"My niece and I served a fancy dinner one night when they had some special company here for the weekend," she continued. With mischief in her voice, she whispered: "They have some very fancy monogrammed towels for the washrooms."

Amy laughed and said: "It sounds like you're getting along famously, Tilly."

"I also wanted to wish you a happy birthday, Miss Amy. Things seem to be working out well for you and I'm glad that you're spending some time with your family. Goodbye, dear."

"Goodbye, Tilly," Amy answered. "It was so thoughtful of you to call." She smiled to herself, glad to hear Tilly's voice and to know that she too was happy.

Amy had a cup of tea and some toast and spent the evening reading a light novel. As she went to sleep, she sighed contentedly. Her family was very dear to her and Tilly had been very considerate to call. She thought about William again and was sure that he would approve of what she was doing with her life.

9

The next morning, Amy was up early as usual, but she noticed after her bath that the water was very slow going down the drain. Her landlady, Mrs. Fillmore, was in the hall downstairs, so she mentioned it to her.

"I'm sorry, dear," she said. "I'll see if I can get my son to come this very morning and fix it." Amy went on her way, confident that everything would be straightened out when she got home.

She arrived at work, and Mr. Carstairs was there already. He greeted her with a smile and asked if she was ready for a busy day. There were many letters to be sent out and much dictation to be done.

"All these people want this work done yesterday," he joked. "By the way, I have to be away at a conference for a week starting on Friday, September thirtieth. That will be one week of your vacation time—paid of course."

"Thank you," she stammered. "That is very good of you."

As it turned out, Amy worked until five-thirty that afternoon. She had picked up some fish-and-chips for dinner and was on her way upstairs when the landlady opened the door and said: "I'm so sorry, Mrs. Somerset, but my son couldn't fix your drain today. A new part will be in tomorrow and it'll be done then. Reginald is a good son but a not-so-good plumber. He has a friend who finally came to help, and found that the new part was needed, but too late in the day."

"Don't worry," said Amy. "I'll have a good wash-up in the morning instead."

"I feel just terrible about this," lamented Mrs. Fillmore. "Would you join us for a cup of tea after dinner?"

Amy didn't really want to, but felt sorry for the older woman who was trying to make amends for the drain problem. She put on a smile and said: "That would be lovely."

"Come down around seven then," beamed the landlady. "I made some fresh cakes today. They're my specialty."

"See you then," answered Amy.

She went upstairs and took off her shoes and washed up in the sink, before eating her fish-and-chips. George was right, they certainly were delicious.

She went downstairs at seven and was greeted with smiles from Mrs. Fillmore, who introduced her to her elderly husband, Donald.

"Sorry, I couldn't help out today, Mrs. Somerset," he said. "I just find those long stairs too much for me. I can still do a few repairs, but my rheumatism is getting worse," he added with a sigh.

"Please sit over here near the fire," gestured Mrs. Fillmore, "and I'll pour the tea." Even though it seemed too warm already, Amy co-operated just to please her.

While Mrs. Fillmore went to the kitchen to get the cakes, her husband said: "You're lucky if you don't get the rheumatism as you get older," and gave a great scowl that reached from his eyebrows to his snowy white hair. "Now my wife has an old recipe she rubs on the sore spots, and it does some good I must admit." Amy smiled in sympathy; she could certainly smell a whiff of the old recipe.

"It interferes with my walking too," he added.

"Now, you still manage to walk down to the Blue Fox on Friday nights for a pint and a game of darts with your old cronies, so you won't get much sympathy, Donald," said Mrs. Fillmore as she passed around the teacakes.

Amy had to press her lips tightly together to prevent herself from laughing out loud. Instead, she said: "This cake looks lovely Mrs. Fillmore. Thank you." She had a few bites of it and added: "No wonder you are famous for your cake. It is certainly delicious!"

Mrs. Fillmore puffed with pride and smiled, saying: "My family always has to have it for tea when they come to visit."

Amy was getting very warm, between the two cups of tea and the heat from the fireplace. She declined another piece of cake or more tea and excused herself. She thanked them for a wonderful time as she went out the door.

"Now your drain will be fixed for you tomorrow for certain, Mrs. Somerset," said Mrs. Fillmore. "I just wanted to add how neatly you keep your flat and how nicely you have finished off the decorations. It's a pleasure to have you for a tenant."

"Thank you again," replied Amy.

She went upstairs and thought how amusing her landlady was, and how very kind.

At noon the next day, she decided to call her dress shop and to speak to Madame Zolie about a skirt to go with her new sweater set. Madame said: "Oh yes, I know exactly what would look good on you." Amy arranged to come in on Saturday.

On Saturday night, she was going to Georgina's for dinner,

and Basil was picking her up. Wanting to look her best, she then called Giorgio, the hairdresser. He told her that she was in luck as he had just had a cancellation for ten o'clock on Saturday, so he would be available.

The afternoon passed quickly as Mr. Carstairs had much dictation for her. She typed up all of his letters before leaving for the day.

As she opened the door of her flat, she wondered what her tub would look like. She was amazed to see a new drain, a clean tub and a freshly scrubbed floor. On her front table was a little note of apology from Mrs. Fillmore and a small plate with two pieces of her famous cake on it.

Amy went downstairs right away, knocked on the Fillmore's door and, with a smile, gave a big thank you and a hug to this kind lady.

"They are good boys," Mrs. Fillmore replied, "and they did all the cleaning up too."

As Amy had a good soak in her restored tub, she mused: I'm actually enjoying my life in London, although I don't know how working mothers manage.

When Basil picked Amy up on Saturday, he gave a low whistle. She admitted to herself vainly that she had done her best with what nature had given her. She felt smart in her fresh hairdo, blue sweater set and short pearls, and the new navy skirt from Madame Zolie's. Even though she did not have a hefty bank balance, she had weakened and put away a two-piece black velvet suit, to be paid in installments by the end of the month.

Georgina greeted her warmly and said: "How marvellous you look, Amy! I believe our London air agrees with you better than the country air." The three of them chattered away for about half an hour and then went in for dinner.

Georgina always insisted on arranging her own flowers. The table had a bouquet of beautiful dahlias in shades of deep pink up to light pink. She was also a member of the Women's League at church that did all the flowers, and she even entered some competitions at the garden shows.

"My, your floral arrangement is one of your best," exclaimed Amy.

They enjoyed an interesting salad, Beef Wellington and crisp vegetables, a sweet, and then crackers and cheeses. After dinner, they returned to the living room to have their tea.

"You mentioned that you have a week's vacation starting September thirtieth," said Georgina. "Would you believe that we have booked a holiday for exactly the same dates? We're renting a villa near St. Raphaël in the south of France. I realize that this is very short notice but Basil and I would be delighted if you would join us.

"Before you answer, let me explain that we've already booked and paid for the villa. It has two bedrooms and even includes a cook and a car and driver. All that you would have to pay would be your airfare and a supplement as a third person to cover the food. It'll be off-season at that time and not only are there no crowds, but the rates are so much more reasonable."

Basil broke in to add: "I refuse to drive on the continent. With all those hair-pin turns and unfamiliar roads, I'm much happier to have a driver included."

Amy was quite speechless but finally managed to say: "I would feel so guilty about intruding on your private holiday."

"Nonsense," replied Georgina. "The truth is that Basil and I frequently go our separate ways while on holiday. I would be delighted to have your companionship. You know how hard solicitors work. Basil's idea of a great holiday is to put his feet up and catch up on his sleep or to read his stuffy old Legal Journals that have sat unread for months on the corner of his desk. He'll probably count this holiday as a great success if he just manages to relax a bit and to forget the office for a week. As for me, I love to explore the shops for local crafts and antiques—none of which holds much interest for him."

Basil added: "Please say yes, Amy. This villa comes highly recommended by friends, and there's plenty of room."

"Well, I don't know what to say. It is very kind of you to ask me to come along."

"Oh, do come Amy," pleaded Georgina.

"I've never been to the south of France so I guess I'd be foolish to say no. Are you sure that you don't mind if I come?"

"No, silly," laughed Georgina. "We'd love to have you with us."

Amy's heart gave a little skip for joy just thinking about it—a new adventure.

"Thank you so much. I would love to join you."

"We must complete our plans next week, and then we'll call you with more details as they're worked out," Georgina replied with a smile.

As Amy prepared for bed that night, she wondered again if she would be imposing on her friends. She only regretted that William was not there to go too. They had made plans to travel when he retired, but it was not to be.

10

Amy had been invited out for dinner on Wednesday evening by Barbara and Jeffery to celebrate Barbara's birthday. She had been a little late coming home, so she rushed to be on time and got to the restaurant by taxi. The grandchildren had been left in the care of a sitter so the adults could have a good conversation. Amy had bought Barbara a subscription to a favourite magazine, so she tucked it in her purse. They were both waiting for her in the restaurant lobby, then all went in to dinner.

Mr. Carstairs was sitting with a lawyer friend at an adjoining table. He gave a little nod to their party and smiled. "I guess we know how to pick the best restaurants," he joked. He wished Barbara a happy birthday when Jeffery told him the reason for their celebration. It was indeed a good restaurant. The meal was superb. Barbara seemed very happy to receive the subscription for her birthday.

Just as they went to get up, Amy's serviette slid to the floor and, as she stooped to pick it up, Mr. Carstairs was there before her. With a gentlemanly bow and a very big smile on his face, he said: "Now, we must solve this small problem of yours, Mrs. Somerset." He laughed heartily and she thanked him despite her embarrassment.

After he had gone, Barbara motioned to her mother and said in a whisper: "That wasn't the worst, Mother. Turn your back to me while I zip up your skirt!"

Horrified, Amy did as she was told, and with an even redder face walked out of the restaurant with them.

"Oh dear!" she cried. "Do you think Mr. Carstairs noticed that? I feel like such a fool. How can I face him tomorrow?"

When they got in the taxi, Barbara started to giggle and then Amy joined in. Soon, all three of them had tears running down their cheeks.

"Why do all these silly things happen when I meet Mr. Carstairs outside the office?" sighed Amy.

"Don't worry, Mother," said Barbara, patting her on the hand, "all he wants is a very efficient secretary, and that's what he has."

The next day was extremely busy, so there was no time on either side to mention the matter.

Her friends, Vivian and Jim Langford, had invited her to come and stay overnight in Ferndene on Saturday. She was looking forward to seeing her former neighbours. Vivian mentioned that Sir John and Lady Beaton had invited them all for tea on Sunday afternoon at two.

On Friday night, Amy packed a few things for her trip and also bought a few groceries for the following week. Amy took the ten-fifteen train the next morning. Vivian and Doctor Jim were there to meet her and she was greeted with hugs and kisses. "My, you look so smart," exclaimed Vivian, "I can tell you've had your hair cut and styled. You've definitely acquired a London polish."

"Oh dear," laughed Amy, "I hope I haven't changed too much!" She looked around at her beloved village and realized how much she missed it.

"Now, we aren't going to run you ragged this weekend," said Jim. "We know how tired you must be after a week's hard work. Here, give me your luggage; my car is just over here."

Vivian looked as happy as ever. Her hair was shining in the sun and she had a rosy glow.

"I didn't know whether you would be here this morning, Doctor Jim. Is your practice still booming?"

"Well, just the usual cuts and bruises, one broken arm, one broken leg and the usual old complaints, real or imaginary—a typical week. Now it remains to be seen how much of your company I get to enjoy."

"I feel very healthy," grinned Amy. "At first, I dragged myself home from the office at night, but now that I'm used to it, it doesn't bother me much."

Soon they were at the house and decided to eat lunch on the terrace, as it was such a delightful day. Their garden looked lovely. It was Vivian's pride. Walter, Tilly's husband, also did a little work in their garden, since Doctor Jim insisted on plenty of fresh vegetables to eat.

Vivian had always loved flowers, so she had a small but enviable perennial garden and in the winter she pored over the garden books and catalogues in anticipation of the spring and summer months. The terrace was in a semi-circle surrounded by raised gardens and a flagstone path led to a large bed of perennials.

Luncheon was a light, delicious salad and some crusty bread, followed by cheese, biscuits and tea.

Vivian made Amy promise to lie down for an hour's rest and

then they would walk to the village. Just then, Doctor Jim got a phone call telling him that old Mrs. Grimsby had sprained her ankle badly, and he felt that he should go and see to it.

"Well, I'll see you at tea hopefully," he said.

Amy piled up some pillows on her bed and covered herself with a downy blanket and had a good nap. Vivian tapped on her door about an hour later as promised; Amy didn't want to ruin her sleep that night. She stretched and said with a smile in her voice: "Oh, how luxurious that was! I'll be down in a few minutes, ready for our walk."

They strolled down the shady lane on their way to Ferndene. The trees were at their best, with glistening green leaves. Some ferns were growing in the wood that they passed and a group of stone and thatched cottages came into view. A stone wall, partly covered with ivy and a few bright flowers in front, protected each cottage. In spite of their similarities, each one had managed to assert its individual dignity by its owner's hand. There were different coloured doors, one had window boxes with flowers, yet another had tubs of flowers or garden chairs. Two young children were sitting on the doorstep of one cottage playing with their much-loved dolls.

Vivian asked about Amy's work as they walked along and whether she saw much of Barbara and Georgina. Amy told her that she did, and that her life in London was very busy. Vivian wanted to go into Mr. Davis's Grocery Store for one or two items.

Suddenly, that familiar loud voice jarred their ears, making them jump—Mrs. Epsom-Smythe. "Well my dear Mrs. Somerset, here for a visit are you? You are looking very well indeed! How are you coping with your new job? Do you find that nasty London smog gets to your lungs? I can never abide it for long; it goes right to my lungs. My husband and I never stay longer than necessary. I have tried to get Lady Jane Beaton to join the Women's Institute, even had her over for tea, but she had some excuses and said perhaps later when she had settled in. Sir John and my husband have played golf at the club a few times. I hope they will become better acquainted. Well, it was nice to see you and have a chat. Mr. Davis, see that my groceries are delivered as soon as possible," she said, glaring at the harassed grocer and striding out the door. "Goodbye, to you both," she added.

"Nothing changes," muttered Mr. Davis. "She thinks I have no other customers but her."

"We didn't really have a chat," laughed Amy. "I never got a chance to say a word."

Mr. Davis laughed too. He served Vivian as she chose some fresh sole for dinner and a crusty loaf of bread.

Doctor Jim didn't return until halfway through tea, saying that poor Mrs. Grimsby did indeed have a bad sprain. He had been forced to call her daughter, who lived in the village too, and ask her to help her mother for the weekend. A daily woman usually came in during the week. Otherwise Mr. Grimsby could only boil water for tea and make toast. He would be no help at all.

Jim had two cups of tea, three sandwiches and two cakes. He had a bit of a paunch and greying hair but his face beamed with kindness and good health. After more conversation and a laugh again about their meeting with Mrs. Epsom-Smythe, they went inside.

About seven, they had a drink of chilled wine while Vivian served pâté and biscuits. Amy insisted on helping to prepare dinner, so she was allowed to make the salad while Vivian prepared the sole.

"I've done enough work today," Jim announced. "You two experts can make dinner while I relax."

Dinner was delicious of course, and there was much hilarity as they all recounted some of the things that had happened since they had last seen each other.

The next morning, they went to St. Boniface for the service and after church, Amy was greeted by many of her old neighbours. Soon it was two o'clock, and teatime with Sir John and Lady Beaton was upon them. As they arrived at Bower House, Amy noted with happiness that the gardens were still showing good bloom despite the lateness of the season, and everything looked so neat.

Tilly opened the door and, oblivious to everyone else, greeted Amy with a hug. "Oh how wonderful to see you again, Miss Amy. You look so cheery, so smart." Sir John and Lady Beaton came into the front hall. "Do come in everyone. It seems rather strange welcoming someone to their very own home," laughed Sir John. "How are you, Doctor Jim, Vivian? Jim and I have met a few times at the golf club, but I'm sure that Jim's practice doesn't permit too many games."

Amy couldn't help glancing around at her beloved home.

"Now we haven't changed much of anything," said Lady Beaton in a brisk, reassuring manner, "just added a few of our own mementoes from abroad. Your house is so tastefully furnished and the garden so nicely maintained that there was not much we wanted to change. Tilly is such a gem and so cheerful; she insisted on serving tea today. I really think she misses you dreadfully. Come and sit down by the window everyone and we shall have tea directly."

Tilly came in all wreathed in smiles and set everything up efficiently. Lady Beaton poured tea and Tilly passed around some of her lovely cakes. Conversation rolled along nicely as they ate the delicious food and drank their tea. When they were finished, they all went out to the terrace and Amy admired the enlarged vegetable garden and the circle of roses.

"Tilly's husband, Walter, is another gem," said Lady Beaton gaily. "We have many vegetables as you see."

Amy's eyes misted over a bit as she thought about the life that she had left behind. Soon they were saying thank you and goodbye. Amy hurried to the kitchen to give Tilly one more hug. "I'll write you another long letter, Tilly."

On her arrival back in London, Amy took a taxi home from the station since she had her bag to carry, but mostly because she was a little weary.

She decided to unpack the bag and to get her clothes out for tomorrow. Then she had a boiled egg, toast and tea for dinner. She also had a relaxing, long soak in the tub and went to bed early with a good novel to read.

As she closed her eyes, she thought about her house. I'm content that Sir Beaton and his wife are taking good care of Bower House, with Tilly's help of course. They are wonderful, caring people.

11

The following week was extra busy, almost erasing the benefit of any rest she had acquired over the weekend. On Wednesday, Mr. Carstairs said he had a heavy load of work to accomplish for tomorrow and asked if she could stay until six-thirty that evening.

"Of course," she replied with a smile. "We'll just make sure to have a good tea at four."

Amy had become very expert at her typing and shorthand and was capable of all that her work entailed. At six-thirty, Mr. Carstairs came out of his office, turning out the light and saying: "Now Mrs. Somerset, if you have nothing else planned, I would like to take you around the corner to that nice café, the Blue Boar, and treat you to a steak and kidney pie. We've done enough work. My butler-cum-chef is off tonight and I hate to eat alone."

At first Amy didn't know what to say, but finally she agreed to go. The owner, knowing Mr. Carstairs by sight, bowed officiously and showed them to a quiet table at the back.

"Something to drink, Mrs. Somerset?" asked Mr. Carstairs.

"Just tea would be fine," she answered with a smile. Mr. Carstairs ordered tea for Amy and ale for himself and asked if she enjoyed steak and kidney pie. She assured him that it was one of her favourites and so he ordered for them both.

When their beverages arrived, Mr. Carstairs asked: "When we're outside the office, may I call you Amy?"

"Please do," she replied.

"I wanted to tell you what a splendid job you are doing. Your secretarial skills are excellent and I appreciate the little touches, like ordering my lunch if I forget, and bringing in those necessary teas."

Amy answered: "I'm enjoying working for you, Mr. Carstairs, although I must admit that I was a little nervous at first."

"Like when you spilled my pencil container on the first day?" he laughed. "Won't you please call me James out of the office? After all, we've known each other for years. We'll reserve our formal names for the office," he said with a twinkle in his blue eyes.

He looks so much younger when he relaxes, thought Amy, and little did she know that James was having the same thoughts about her.

"What have you been doing on weekends?" he asked. "I've been meeting you here and there a great deal. We seem to have similar tastes in entertainment and dining."

As they ate their excellent pie and salad, Amy told him about her weekend—staying at the Langfords' house in Ferndene. She also told him about having tea at her own home with Sir John and Lady Jane Beaton.

"They're keeping it in lovely shape and seem to enjoy it as much as I did. Thank you again for recommending them to me."

"As I told you, Sir John is an old chum of mine. We belong to the same club and I would vouch for his character thoroughly. I'm glad things have worked out for you."

"My friend, Tilly, who has worked for our family for many years, has stayed on to help them."

He replied: "I think it's wonderful that things have worked out so well for all of us."

The next day, she had lunch in the cafeteria with Josie. The young girl had more colour in her cheeks now and seemed to be returning to her normal self.

Josie said: "I try to remember what you said about keeping busy. It really does seem to help a lot."

Amy replied: "I know that your heart is still broken and will take a long time to mend. Now that I'm working, I find that two or three days go by when I have no time to think about my sorrow. I can even feel some happiness occasionally."

On Friday night, Georgina called to talk about their plans for the much-anticipated visit to the south of France. "The flight leaves at eight next Saturday morning and we'll be met by our driver in Nice on our arrival. There'll be so many lovely things to see and do!"

"Barbara and Jeffery have offered to take me to the airport because of the very early flight time, and I'm going to their house for dinner this Sunday," said Amy.

They spent a few minutes discussing their wardrobes and how excited they were, and planned to speak again on Wednesday.

On the week-end, Amy went through her wardrobe and

washed some things and took others to the dry cleaners. She also needed a few groceries for the coming week.

Amy was becoming familiar with the community near her flat. The grocer, a white-haired gentleman named Mr. Nazir, ran the store along with his wife and daughter. Amy had introduced herself to them and they familiarly called each other by name.

His wife, Fatima, made all the baked goods and meat pies and fresh salads. Many business people stopped by after work to buy these items for dinner. Their daughter, Nina, a clever girl with wavy black hair and a winning smile, totalled up the groceries and carefully packed them in bags.

Mr. Nazir proudly told Amy that his daughter had suggested selling plants and flowers, which also decorated the outside of the store.

Amy went into the store often for some of these items, especially a prepared meal when she was too tired to cook after work. As well, there was a same-day dry cleaner, which was handy, and a chemist, which she rarely used. The bus stopped down at the corner and the driver always gave her a friendly nod when he saw her. It was indeed like a miniature village.

Amy had paid off her new suit at Madame Zolie's and bought a lovely print sundress on sale. Amy's bank balance was mounting quickly in spite of paying her rent, buying food and the few clothes necessary for her job. It gave her a smile of satisfaction to add her two weeks' wages to the total. I still have to pay for my airplane ticket and get some traveller's cheques, she thought. I'm sure that Georgina and I still have much to talk about.

A few days before her holiday, James mentioned that he was already booked for the conference at a seaside resort. He asked what her plans were and, with a very surprised look on his face commented: "My dear Amy, you are full of surprises. I envy you that wonderful holiday. I went to the south of France about twenty years ago with some old cronies and it is indeed a marvellous place for a holiday. Basil and Georgina will be excellent company. Now, there I will be, listening to some old bore lecturing everyone, while you're having such a good time. I'm feeling very sorry for myself now, even though I do have a couple of golf games lined up. We will compare notes when you return."

The rest of the week passed quickly and Amy packed and re-packed her suitcase several times, changing her mind about what she should bring.

12

Barbara and Jeffery picked up Amy and drove her to the airport early on Saturday morning. Amy's heart was beating rapidly, firstly in anticipation, and secondly because she had not been on a plane in about three years. She had gone to Holland with William just before he fell ill. They had enjoyed it very much and had hoped to go on many more trips.

Luckily, Georgina, Basil and Amy were seated together and Amy hung onto Georgina for reassurance as the plane took off for Nice.

"There now, relax Amy. We're on our way. Basil has promised to take good care of us. He is fluent in French you know, since he often does business in Paris; that should make things easier."

Upon their arrival in Nice, they were met by a short, thin man with a little moustache, who jumped out of a beautiful black Citroën and introduced himself as "Antoine." He had been watching for the trio, and efficiently took their bags and stowed them away. He spoke very good English.

Antoine explained the beauties of Nice as they ascended into the hills above the beautiful, blue "Baie des Anges." You could look down and see the marina with tiny-looking boats lined up in rows.

"Isn't this marvellous?" exclaimed Georgina.

"The view certainly is spectacular," agreed Basil.

Amy felt too breathless with excitement to do anything but just smile and nod in agreement. Antoine headed towards Haut-des-Cagnes, which he explained was a major artist colony, made famous by Renoir. After that came Antibes with its famed old harbour and many large, modern yachts.

"Oh, I wish I could take pictures of all this," said Georgina impatiently.

"We will be back this way, Madame, during the week, when you have more time. Right now, my wife will be waiting to serve you lunch at the villa." Onwards he drove to Cannes where, from another magnificent aspect, they could see the islands of Ste. Marguerite and Ste. Honorat which he pointed out to them.

"You must take a boat trip, and picnic on the islands," said Antoine.

They all agreed it was another thing they would like to do. Cannes was known as one of the famous playgrounds of Europe and many charming sights were to be seen.

"If you choose, we will return here this week and I will be happy to show you some of the highlights," said Antoine. "The true Côte d'Azur begins here in St. Raphaël," he added, as they approached the rugged coast dotted with much red rock.

"I will bring you down to the town tomorrow if you wish, but now we are near the end of our journey," he announced.

They all looked at each other in delight and anticipation as they climbed up and up a rather rugged road. The much-awaited villa was charming. It was rose-coloured with wrought-iron gates and had a flagstone patio with pots of flowers everywhere.

The patio was surrounded by a wall with pink bougainvillea spilling over the top.

A rosy-cheeked woman with dark hair and eyes came shyly towards them. Antoine came over to her and putting his arm around her and, gently pushing her forward, introduced her as his wife, Claudette.

"Bonjour, bonjour, mesdames et monsieur. I will be helping in the house this week to make you more comfortable and cook your meals. Please come in."

She led them into the house through a dark red-tiled hallway into a bright living room that was centered on a glorious view of the Mediterranean. Three comfortable chairs, a large leather sofa and a large table were the furniture in the room. A beautiful rose carpet glowed on the floor. The dining area had a lovely view looking out a bow window at the front terrace and beyond that, the sea.

They all exclaimed over these beautiful rooms, and drifted as one to the terrace overlooking the Mediterranean. It was protected by a low wall and set with patio furniture. The lounge chairs looked particularly tempting.

"I think I've died and gone to heaven," sighed Georgina. "I had no idea it would be this wonderful." They all agreed.

"Would you like to unpack your belongings and see your quarters now?" asked Claudette.

Georgina and Basil were shown to a lovely bedroom which had wrought-iron shuttered windows overlooking the sea, a large bed, an armoire, a desk and a chair. Amy's bedroom was on the other side of the living room, and furnished with a similar flair

"If you would like to refresh yourselves," announced Claudette, "lunch will be served in half an hour."

Amy couldn't decide whether she was tired or hungry, and

decided she was both. She had been up since six, too excited to sleep any more.

She found her bedroom very charming and comfortable. The large arched window had a cushioned seat beneath it and overlooked the sea. The other window towards the front courtyard had pretty wrought-iron work on it. A cozy armchair with a side table and an armoire and a comfortable-looking bed, piled with soft pillows, completed the furnishings.

Amy hung up her clothes and put some loose items in the two drawers at the bottom. It seemed so warm that she decided to change into a cool sundress and sandals.

As she came out of her room, she laughed, noting that Georgina and Basil had changed into cooler clothes too.

"Isn't this the most marvellous place?" exclaimed Amy. "It is truly a bit of paradise."

"I'm really hungry," said Basil. "I hope we're eating lunch right away. Wasn't it wonderful to have Antoine as a driver? I wouldn't have enjoyed negotiating some of those hair-pin turns."

Claudette came out of the kitchen and invited them to sit on the patio for lunch. She had put out blue placemats and set a vase of pink flowers as a centrepiece.

She had made a famous local dish—Salade Niçoise. Antoine poured each of them a glass of chilled white wine. The salad combined boiled baby potatoes, green beans, torn lettuce, wedges of tomatoes, hard-boiled eggs, some chunk white tuna, anchovy filets, red onion and black olives. The dressing was a wine vinegar and olive oil mixture. Amy took detailed mental notes on this, because it was one of the most enjoyable salads that she had ever eaten.

They all raved over the salad and the chilled wine and soon were sitting back with sighs of contentment.

"Well, this is certainly more than I ever hoped for," commented Georgina.

After the meal, they looked at each other's rooms and examined the bright living room again with its rustic fireplace and easy chairs and its lovely bowed window in front. Claudette showed them the cheerful kitchen with the spacious sink, the butcher-block counters and modern appliances. Geraniums grew in pots on the windowsill.

"My husband, Antoine, and I enjoy running this villa and we have a nice set of rooms over the garage," she said with a smile. "I will be here when you need me. Just let me know which meals you wish me to serve."

Amy exclaimed: "That was the most delicious salad I've ever had, Claudette. You called it Salade Niçoise? I was trying to identify all the ingredients that were in it. Perhaps you could write it down for me sometime this week?"

Claudette thanked her for the compliment.

Basil told the girls they could do what they wanted, but he was going to have a short nap. He begged Georgina not to let him sleep longer than one hour. Amy and Georgina decided to sit on the terrace on two cushioned lounges in the dappled shade, and enjoy the stunning view. The sea was a sparkling aqua and the town below comprised mostly of white buildings. They both commented on how beautiful everything was and how they were looking forward to the rest of the week.

After they had chatted for a while, Georgina said that she must wake up Basil.

"He's as grumpy as a bear after he wakes up. He works so hard however and does need his rest." Amy closed her eyes for a few minutes and her friends returned, teasing each other.

"Basil is trying to set up our week at a very strenuous pace.

Please talk to Antoine first, and get his recommendations, darling. Let's do our sight-seeing just part days, please."

Basil went off to find Antoine and soon returned. He informed the ladies that Antoine would take them all down to St. Rafaël for the eleven o'clock service tomorrow, and then to a café for lunch. After church, they could explore the town for a while and be picked up at four. On Monday, if the weather was nice, they could go to Cannes, take a boat to the islands and have a picnic there.

"We'll go along with your decisions, dear," laughed Georgina, "won't we Amy? I for one am starting to feel too lazy already to even care."

They sat on the terrace until dusk and then went in to spruce up for dinner. They each put a sweater over their shoulders. Since the view from the terrace was too magnificent to miss on their first night, they opted to eat right there. The lights twinkled like stars below in the town while the stars started to come out in the heavens at the same time. The flowers in their tubs gave off a sweet perfume adding to the perfection.

"I have made a pot-au-feu," said Claudette, as she brought a bubbling casserole to the table. It smelled so delicious. The usual crusty bread accompanied the meal only this time Antoine poured a mellow red wine. The stew had a rich-tasting beef gravy with a touch of wine and garlic along with tender baby vegetables.

"After our huge salad at lunch," laughed Basil, "I never thought I would be hungry again." He ended up having two huge helpings plus a large dish of crème caramel. "We had better do some walking tomorrow," he groaned.

Sunday dawned sunny and bright. The air was balmy and it caressed their faces with a light breeze. They ate a light breakfast of fruit, croissants and coffee, and Antoine drove them down into St. Raphaël. He said that he would pick them up after the service and drive them to a small café where he had made a luncheon reservation in their name.

True to his word, Antoine was waiting, wreathed in smiles when the service was over.

He knew the owner of this delightful café overlooking the harbour and their table was reserved as promised. Antoine gave them a map where he had marked out different attractions so that they wouldn't get lost. "I will be at the car as marked on the map, at four o'clock, my friends," he said. "Au revoir."

Georgina, Basil and Amy's table was protected by a colourful umbrella, and they were delighted by the waving palms and the many flowers. The sea was so blue it was indescribable.

"I keep pinching myself to see if this is really true," said Amy with awe.

"Well, at this rate, you'll be black and blue by the end of the week," laughed Georgina.

After a leisurely lunch and much amusing conversation, they set out to walk up and down the quaint streets, and looked in some of the interesting shops. Amy and Georgina insisted that they must have a sunhat and sunglasses for tomorrow's boat ride. Basil said: "I'll buy some sunglasses too, but forget the hat."

They had a fun time trying on different hats, even trying to talk Basil into a French beret. He put one on and struck a serious pose, which moved the girls to hysterical laughter. After exchanging much advice on which sunglasses were most suitable, Basil helped figure out the money and they left the shop quite satisfied.

At about three o'clock, they discovered an interesting antique shop. It was not in very tidy order, but that added to its charm. They were all busy browsing when Amy discovered an intriguing and colourful oil painting in an ornate antique frame hidden behind a larger picture on the floor. She picked it up for a closer look. It was a Mediterranean scene, a tapestry of colours of blue, rose, green and white with some pale yellow. She caught her breath as she looked it over. It was signed A.A. Lebrandt and although it was a little dusty, the painting depicted the area beautifully.

I've never heard of this painter, she said to herself, but I'm very attracted to his work.

She quietly showed it to Georgina who admired it as well. Amy also showed the picture to Basil. He said casually to the owner: "We found this old painting tucked away at the back under another larger painting. There's no price tag on it."

The owner examined the painting carefully, looked Basil straight in the eye and said in French: "You have very good taste, monsieur. This artist enjoys some fame in this area and his works command good prices."

Basil negotiated with the old man at some length and finally a sum was reached that seemed very fair indeed. Amy agreed. The owner wrapped it up for her and she walked out of the shop feeling as if she had bought a Renoir for just a few hundred francs.

"Oh Basil, thank you. Whatever you said to him has given me a painting that I am sure to treasure."

"Let's look at it again when we get home. I know a chap in London who could be trusted to get it cleaned and evaluated for you."

They easily found Antoine and the car waiting for them.

As soon as they returned to the villa, Amy unwrapped her small painting. They crowded around it and declared it to be charming and an astute purchase.

"Now leave it to me to speak to my friend in London about

cleaning it up. You will find that the colours will look much brighter and the frame too," said Basil. "This piece is obviously an original, but it reminds me of another painting that I've seen before."

They all had a rest on the terrace again, too tired to even speak for a while. They watched dusk creep slowly over the scene and saw that Claudette was setting up a beautiful table inside complete with flowers and candles. They washed and changed and sat down to a lovely dinner of Sole Florentine with tiny vegetables surrounding it. For dessert, they had a chocolate mousse.

"Oh, this is wonderful," sighed Georgina, "I wish we could stay for a month!"

"We would each gain ten pounds," laughed Basil.

"Oh how true," agreed Amy, trying to puff out her cheeks to show that it had happened already.

In the morning, the sea looked like glass and Antoine pronounced it a perfect day to go by boat to the islands. Claudette packed a basket lunch for them while they chose their wardrobe for the day.

Antoine drove them to the marina. It took half an hour to sail to St. Honorat. The girls were glad to have their sun hats tied on. The sea was lovely with hues of blue and green. Soon the pine woods were visible. As the passengers disembarked, each group headed off to explore the island and to find comfortable and scenic picnic sites.

Georgina, Basil and Amy found a spot under the cool trees and not too far from the sea, so that they could feel the light breeze. After laying out a couple of blankets and talking languidly among themselves, they decided to open the hamper and see what lunch had been packed. There were some crusty bread rolls, pâté, some soft ripe cheese, fresh fruit and a decanter of Antoine's home-made white wine.

"That was so delicious," declared Georgina, as they finished. "It must taste extra good because of the wonderful salt air."

"Well, if you ladies don't mind, that lunch has made me feel awfully sleepy," yawned Basil. With that, he curled up on his side on the blanket and was soon fast asleep. The girls smiled at each other as they cleaned up and moved to another patch of shade to have a quiet conversation.

They observed a lady throwing a ball about for her little poodle. He was chasing it happily back and forth under the trees. All of a sudden, the ball ricocheted off one of the trees and landed right in the crook of Basil's arm. The poodle immediately came racing over, barking and growling at Basil, who sat up abruptly, wondering dazedly what in the world was going on. He had the quick presence of mind to pick up the precious ball and to throw it away. The lady spoke loudly and animatedly in French and Basil, ever the perfect gentleman, calmed her down as he got up.

Georgina and Amy had watched all this with some trepidation, lest Basil be bitten, then with some concern as the woman seemed to berate Basil. They didn't understand what she was saying and tried to hide their amusement until it was over. When she was out of sight, they all laughed heartily although Basil was still a little upset at being awakened so rudely.

"Oh darling, you always end up being the gentleman. That's one of the things I love about you," laughed Georgina.

Soon, they noticed dark clouds scudding across the sky and the wind picking up. They decided to return to the mainland. They managed to get on board the boat as soon as it docked. The waves were a little choppy and, after a half-hour's boat ride, they found their stomachs a little queasy. Fortunately, Antoine had noticed the weather too and was there in the car to greet them.

They just arrived back at the villa when the rains swept in from the sea. Claudette shut everything up tightly and they felt comfortable and secure.

That evening, Claudette outdid herself with an excellent veal dinner done with mushrooms and wine sauce. She had also made a fruit pudding topped with brandied sauce and everyone felt satisfied and relaxed. They were tired after such a busy day, and after laughing again over Basil's little episode, they said good night.

Basil chose to stay at the villa to do some reading the next day. Antoine drove the ladies to Cannes for a day of sightseeing. The weather had cleared overnight and the sparkling blue sky and the turquoise sea beckoned anew.

Antoine had suggested a ride on the funicular up to Super-Cannes. The view was superb even though Amy was a little nervous about the height. After a lunch on the famous seaside promenade where Amy ordered her favourite Salade Niçoise, they went to the Musée de la Castre with its anthropology collections and then strolled among the lovely gardens adorned with palm trees.

They returned to the villa foot-sore but very pleased and each took a hot soak in a tub. Dinner was served on the patio overlooking the town and they sighed again with marvel as evening fell and the lights glittered below.

The next morning, they all felt lazy, so they lounged about until after lunch and then went again to St. Raphaël and walked about. They took special joy in the small beaches and the wonderful vistas that presented themselves at every turn.

Thursday dawned bright and beautiful again and Antoine

took them to Grasse, the centre of the world's perfume-making industry. The fields made a tapestry of colour everywhere and there were many fragrant wildflowers, especially lavender. They visited a perfume factory, which was truly fascinating. Of course, the women each bought a bottle of perfume produced there. The old part of town, especially the cathedral, was also worth visiting.

Amy, Georgina and Basil were all tired by mid-afternoon, so they asked Antoine to drive them back to the villa. They rested on the patio before changing for dinner.

Claudette had made a wonderful Beef Bourguignon for dinner, followed by Gateau St. Honoré. They all threw caution to the winds and had two helpings of this fabulous dessert.

Their last full day was also bright and warm. After discussing possible excursions, they agreed unanimously that the most enjoyable and sensible thing to do was to simply stay at their luxurious villa and to pack up for their departure on Saturday.

Amy thought to herself: I have amassed so many happy memories and have taken many pictures. They'll make a wonderful album of the trip that I've shared with good friends.

The next morning, Antoine took them on the beautiful scenic drive back to the airport in Nice. Amy had decided to include the painting in her carry-on luggage. She and Georgina even wore their sun hats like real tourists, loath to leave them behind.

Amy felt braver about the plane ride home, but still held onto Georgina's arm as the plane took off and landed. They shared a taxi ride home, Amy's flat being not too much out of the way. She hugged each of them as they said goodbye and she thanked them profusely for including her in their wonderful holiday. Basil promised once again to give her the name of the art restorer.

Amy sighed happily as she started up the stairs. Just then, the landlady's door opened and her kindly old face appeared.

"Just getting home dear? Did you have a good time?"

"Oh, it was delightful," Amy answered. "I'll tell you all about it as soon as I get my photos and souvenirs organized."

After unpacking, a hot bath and a light meal, she was asleep early. Her own bed felt so comfortable.

13

On Monday morning, Amy arrived at the office early only to find James already working away at his desk.

"Ah, Mrs. Somerset," he cried. "I am so glad to see you. How was your holiday? I can see by your bright smile and happy, relaxed look that you enjoyed it."

"Oh yes," she replied with enthusiasm. "The three of us had the most perfect villa with a delightful view, and most glorious weather."

"Now you're making me very jealous, you know," he laughed. "There I was last week at this boring conference, one golf game rained out and scoring miserably in the other."

He made a pouty face and she laughed out loud.

"I would like to take you out for dinner later this week and hear all about it. I told you that I had been to the French Riviera about twenty years ago, and it would revive some fond memories for me. Right now, there's a sizeable stack of correspondence on my desk and that means we have a lot of work to do."

She reverted immediately to her brisk office manner, which

made him laugh. They managed to do a very good day's work indeed.

Amy got off the bus feeling very tired. She stopped at the grocer's to pick up a few necessary items and a hot meat pie. She also had cleaning to pick up and treated herself to a fresh bouquet of flowers.

Later in the week, Basil called to give her the name of the art restorer. On her lunch hour, she took her small painting to him and was told that he would need two weeks to clean it and prepare a valuation.

James asked her to go with him to one of his favourite restaurants for dinner on the Friday night. She was encouraged to leave work at four, as he did also. She had a quick hairdo by Giorgio at the salon and decided to wear her new suit. Her simple pearl earrings set it off beautifully. She made sure that all buttons and zippers were done up.

James picked her up in a taxi at six-thirty. He had made a reservation and since he knew the owner, they were soon seated in a comfortable booth in a quiet corner. As they were handed the menu, James asked if she would like sherry or wine.

"Wine please," she answered. "Strange, but sherry goes right to my head."

He laughed and said he must remember that.

"I must tell you again how well you look after your holiday. I have been quite a taskmaster this week with all the work that had to be done. I admire your competence and appreciate how much easier it makes my daily life."

"The job has been good for me too," she replied.

Over shrimp cocktail, he asked Amy to tell him all about her trip. She tried to remember all they had done and seen. She related some amusing adventures too, and told him of the painting she had bought. When the main course came, she recounted the story of the poodle waking Basil from his nap at their picnic. At this, James laughed and laughed.

"Oh dear," he chuckled, "I can just picture him."

As they finished their dinner and had their coffee, he said: "You know, I could leave my stuffy work tomorrow and start off on some new adventures. You've made your trip very real to me. Thank you."

As they got up to leave, Amy's napkin slid off her lap to the floor. Her face turned scarlet as James picked it up and handed it to her with a bow.

"Thank you," she said in a small voice.

After they got into the taxi, they looked at each other—James with a questioning lift to his eyebrows and a hint of a smile at the edge of his mouth. They both broke into laughter.

"You must think me a very inept person sometimes," laughed Amy. "You always see me outside the office doing something very, very …"

"No, my dear, you are very charming. Don't ever change."

As Amy got out at her flat, she thanked him for a wonderful evening and said a heartfelt goodbye.

I feel like a gawky teenager, she mused to herself. What's the matter with me? Could it be an attraction to him?

Barbara, Jeffery and the children were anxious to see her, so she had been asked to join them for Sunday lunch. Jeffery insisted on picking her up as they had decided to go to service at the church together first. She was greeted with many hugs and kisses, which made her feel very loved indeed. The children insisted on sitting on either side of her during the service and they all enjoyed the organ music and the choir.

After a delicious lunch, Amy displayed some of the many souvenirs she had bought and an album of her pictures.

"Grandmother, it must have been so beautiful there!" exclaimed Stephanie. "Thanks for the postcards."

"How good you look, Mother," said Barbara. "Your vacation certainly agreed with you."

Amy recounted some of their adventures and some of the funny things that happened. They too laughed over Basil's encounter with the poodle.

"Imagine having two people to take care of you," added Barbara. "Such luxury!"

"Were you afraid to fly again, Grandmother?" asked George.

"Trust you to find my weakness, dearest," laughed Amy. "I felt anxious at first, but I hung onto Georgina's arm and that helped me during the takeoffs and landings."

"I've never been in an airplane yet, but I certainly would like to soon," he added, looking hopefully at his parents.

"Well, your mother and I are talking about a family trip to France next summer," said Jeffery. "We'll have to discuss it some more."

Amy mentioned that James Carstairs had taken her out for dinner on Friday night because he wanted to hear about her trip. He had been to the Riviera twenty years ago.

Barbara and Jeffery exchanged questioning glances. Amy told them about the small painting she had found in the antique store and how Basil had recommended it be cleaned by a friend of his who was an art restorer.

"It could be worth millions of pounds, Grandmother!" exclaimed George. "Some very famous artist might have painted it."

"I don't think so," she replied, "but the colours are very lovely and the picture has the look and feel of southern France."

Amy smiled brightly, as she hugged and kissed each of them. "I must be on my way now, my dears. Thank you so much. It has been wonderful to see all of you again."

The art restorer called a few days later to say that her painting was ready to be picked up. One day, while James was out for lunch with a client, she quickly walked the two blocks from the office to the restorer's gallery.

"Your painting is quite wonderful. The colours are brilliant, yet so harmonious," he told her. "I must tell you, Mrs. Somerset, that you made a great bargain in buying this painting. It is appraised at seventeen hundred pounds."

"Oh my goodness!" she cried in a shocked voice. "I had no idea. I just liked the painting. Oh my! You have done a wonderful job restoring it. Thank you."

She paid him by cheque and took the carefully wrapped parcel back to the office.

Amy ate her sandwich and drank her tea deep in thought. When James returned, he spied the wrapped painting against the wall near her desk.

"Is this the painting you told me about?" he asked. "Would you mind showing it to me?"

Amy carefully unwrapped it and held it in the sunlight for him to see. He seemed dumbfounded for a moment, not saying a word. He peered at the signature—"A.A. Lebrandt."

"Well, well," he said. "Twenty years ago when I went on my holiday to the south of France, I too bought a painting about this size, and by the same artist."

"What?" she exclaimed. "Surely it isn't exactly the same."

"Oh no," he laughed, "but the colours and style are unmistakable."

"May I tell you what the painting is worth?" she asked.

"The restorer has given you an appraisal then?"

"Oh yes—seventeen hundred pounds!" she answered smugly and with much happiness.

James joined in her happiness. "Well, we both have a good eye for a bargain. Congratulations! I wish that you could see my painting. It's hanging at home. As a matter of fact, I'm having Basil and Georgina for a drink at my house and taking them to dinner a week from Saturday. I would like to show my painting to all of you. Please come. As you know, I like to entertain each of the partners personally at least once a year."

Amy answered: "I would love to see your painting and compare it to my purchase."

"I'm sure it will be a very enjoyable evening for you, too."

For the rest of the week, it was back to business.

Of course she had to call Barbara and Georgina with the good news about her painting. They were both very happy for her.

She arranged a nice grouping over the mantelpiece featuring her painting in the middle, a pair of silver candlesticks on one side and a ceramic bird on the other.

On Saturday, she invited Barbara and her family as well as Georgina and Basil for tea at her flat and to show off her bargain. She had to borrow a couple of folding chairs from her landlady, who had peeked in to see the painting earlier in the week and who insisted on sending up two of her special cakes to serve at the party.

Amy gave her a hug and laughed: "Now how fortunate I am, Mrs. Fillmore, to have someone as sweet as you are for a landlady and a friend. Thank you." Mrs. Fillmore hugged her back saying: "It's our pleasure to have you, Mrs. Somerset."

At Saturday's tea, everyone raved over the restored painting. Basil and Georgina were enraptured over the colours and how they had been made to look more brilliant.

"Even the gold frame seems to glow," said Barbara in awe.

"And it's worth seventeen hundred pounds!" shouted George in triumph. Everyone looked at Amy, who seemed rather perturbed that this secret was out.

"George, remember your manners, my boy," said Jeffery with a frown. The boy looked rather sheepish. Everyone started to laugh and to congratulate Amy on her bargain, and the moment passed.

Her sitting room was crowded, but no one seemed to care. The cakes were delicious, and Stephanie felt very grown up being allowed to pass out the plates. Three pots of tea and two plates of sandwiches were soon gone and everyone was quite satisfied.

"Mother, your flat is so bright and you've made it so homey. You must be very happy here," said Barbara.

"Oh yes," she answered. "If one has to live in London, you couldn't ask for a better situation. I have a wonderful landlady and the flat is also convenient to the bus and the shops."

"Especially the fish-and-chips shop," chirped George.

"Oh George, you think of nothing but your stomach," laughed Stephanie.

Soon everyone said their thank yous and goodbyes and, with a last look at the painting, they took their leave.

14

The following Saturday was the day of James Carstairs' dinner. Georgina had arranged for both she and Amy to have their hair and nails done in the morning at Giorgio's. He made them both look beautiful of course and he, as always, praised his own work.

Amy had decided to wear a long velvet skirt and simple satin blouse with her pearls. Mother always said to dress quietly, but in good taste, she thought.

Basil and Georgina picked her up in a taxi. At James's house, the butler opened the door and took their wraps as their host appeared and greeted each of them with a pleasant smile and a "Good evening."

James does indeed look handsome tonight, Amy thought as he showed to advantage in a navy suit and shimmery grey tie.

"Please come in," he said, leading them to his elegant living room. As she did so, Amy's eyes flew to the beautiful picture over the mantelpiece. She drew in her breath, seeing immediately the resemblance in colour and style to her own painting.

"My dear friends, Amy is looking at my painting which is by A.A. Lebrandt, the same artist as the canvas that she just recently purchased with your assistance in the south of France."

They were amazed at the close similarities. His painting had more of the sea and sky, while hers had more landscape. As drinks were served, they talked about the paintings and Amy and James were congratulated on their purchases. James recounted how he had found his painting in a similar back-street shop about twenty years before.

"My art expert figures that it was painted about sixty years ago. We're going to have to delve into this more deeply, Amy."

They were whisked off in a taxi to the restaurant. It had a canopied ceiling and lovely old paintings on the walls. A fresh bouquet was in the centre of the large table. There was much discussion over the menu and advice from the waiter on the specials for the evening. At last, all was decided and they relaxed over a glass of wine.

James was a marvellous host, including each person in the conversation and drawing him or her out, as well as entertaining them with a few lawyer-like stories. Amy did indeed feel very relaxed and was beginning to know her boss outside the office and better see his private self.

Christmas was coming and Amy had been invited to Barbara's for a few days. Also, an office party consisting of the partners and the secretaries was being held in the cafeteria. Amy had tried to do a bit of shopping but didn't know whether it was appropriate to buy something for James. In the end, she found a book on artists of southern France, and A.A. Lebrandt was mentioned in it a few times.

The children had a list of things they wanted and with Barbara's advice, that shopping was easy to do. She had a lovely picture from the trip enlarged and framed as a gift for Georgina and Basil. For Barbara, she bought a beautiful evening bag; and for Jeffery, a cuff link box made out of various woods.

The last day of the week arrived and the office party was set to start at noon with a catered lunch. Before going down, she presented James with his book. He was very appreciative and remarked that she must have put much time and thought into the gift. With that, he pressed an envelope into her hand containing a pair of symphony tickets.

She thanked him sincerely. "These tickets are wonderful. Perhaps Barbara will enjoy going to the symphony with me," she added.

"You have done more for me than anyone could ever have imagined. Thank you again very much," he said with a smile.

They walked downstairs side-by-side. All the staff ate and chatted with one another, Amy taking a few minutes to talk to Josie who was having a large dinner with her family on Christmas. James was going to visit his sister and her family who lived out of town. He stated that he expected Amy to enjoy the week's holiday while he was away. She told him that she would be with Barbara's family. Everyone parted in a seasonal mood.

On Christmas Eve, Amy went to stay with Barbara and the family. She was looking forward to the festivities. Amy had also sent a note to Tilly and Walter, accompanied by a lovely package.

Stephanie and George greeted her with "Merry Christmas, Grandmother," and many hugs and kisses. She could tell they were very excited.

"Come and see our tree. We just have a few more ornaments to put on. Would you like to help?" The children were jumping up and down. Amy was greeted affectionately by Barbara and Jeffery who helped her with her armful of packages.

She then helped put a few more Christmas balls on the tree while carols played in the background.

"Shall I play you the two new carols on the piano that I've learned for Christmas?" asked Stephanie.

"Oh, I would love to hear them, dear," replied Amy.

Stephanie was very proud to play her pieces without a mistake and Amy clapped for her and gave her some kisses.

"Very well done, dear."

"Mother has made a French dinner tonight. I hope we like it," added George.

Amy laughed. "I am sure we will, George."

Dinner did indeed turn out to be delicious. Barbara had tourtière with homemade rhubarb chutney on the side, which she had made last spring, and a generous salad.

"Perhaps when the children are a little older, we'll go to midnight service," said Jeffery, "but for now we'll go to the morning choral service. Christmas is a busy and exciting day for the children and they'll be up early."

"But that means we don't get to open our gifts until after," moaned George.

"You do get to have your stocking gifts, which are always on your bed. Now, be off to bed early you two." Everyone put their gifts under the tree and the adults went to bed early too.

You couldn't help but hear the children on Christmas morning. Stephanie had gone into George's room to show him the contents of her stocking. Barbara finally said that they might as well all get up and have a quick breakfast in their bathrobes.

Church service was at nine-thirty, so they left early to be there on time. The choir, consisting of young boys was indeed delightful with their clear soprano voices. Stephanie and George could hardly contain themselves as they waited for their father to turn on the Christmas tree lights and to open the living room doors. The children tore through their gifts with screams of surprise and joy.

Barbara and Jeffery had given Stephanie a most beautiful doll from France, which she promptly named "Josette". She also received a board game, some clothes and a silver bracelet.

Amy had chosen for her a jewellery box with a ballerina on top. When it was opened, it played a lively song from *The Nutcracker*. Stephanie was delighted.

George found a new train set behind the tree. This was a complete set with flashing signals, rising barriers and landscaping. He immediately wanted his father to help him set it up in his room.

"Open up your other gifts first," suggested Jeffery, "and then we can spend a while together before lunch, playing engineer."

George also got a building set, and another board game. He barely looked at his new shirt and socks and cast them aside. Like most boys, he wasn't really interested in clothes for a gift.

Amy had bought him a hand-held electronic game which gave off many annoying, loud noises. George was thrilled with his gift and played with it immediately. He thanked everyone for their gifts and gave hugs to each. As he made his game start again, Amy laughed and said: "I think we might regret my purchase by the end of the day".

They all cried out for Amy to open her pile of gifts. The children had bought her a pair of gloves, with their own money they emphasized! Barbara and Jeffery had given her a soft pink cashmere cardigan.

"Oh my goodness, you are all too good to me," she sniffed with tears in her eyes, and kissed them all.

Barbara remarked: "You seem to be getting a lot of wear out

of your other sweaters, so we bought you a new one, Mother."

Barbara and Jeffery seemed to truly like their gifts, so Amy was content.

Dinner was served at two o'clock and the table seemed to groan under the weight of all the food. The meal consisted of the traditional roast turkey and plum pudding. After dinner, they were groaning too, saying they had eaten too much. Each person had opened a cracker and all laughed at each other's paper hats.

George and Jeffery disappeared after dinner to play with the train, and Barbara said with a laugh: "Well, whenever those two disappear, I will always know where they are".

Stephanie was quietly playing in the corner with Josette and her music box. This gave Barbara and Amy a chance to have a good long talk and Barbara remarked again on how well things had worked out for her mother.

Amy said: "Now that I'm getting to know James better, I'm not as nervous around him as I was in the beginning. He is actually a very gentle, generous and humourous man. He works much too hard of course, as I fully know, but I feel quite capable of handling the work.

Barbara was interested to hear Amy's assessment of her boss and this served to reinforce the questions that had been going through her mind.

Boxing Day was another holiday, so the children played with their toys and high tea was served, with mince pies, fruitcake and scones, port wine and tea. Amy stayed two more days but then went home to prepare for New Year's Eve celebration which was to be with Georgina and Basil at their home.

They picked her up early in the afternoon on New Year's Eve day and went out to dinner at a fine restaurant where they enjoyed a delicious meal. Back at Georgina and Basil's, they tried to keep a lively conversation going so that they would all make it to midnight.

"Oh," groaned Amy, "who is going to be able to stay awake until midnight?"

"Well, we dare not tell any of our friends that we went to bed before ringing in the New Year," laughed Basil, "so we'll have to tough it out."

They sipped at their champagne and Basil entertained them with some funny stories and as the bells in the city rang out, they hugged and kissed each other, wishing one another a Happy New Year.

"Now we can go to bed, Amy," yawned Georgina.

The next morning, being a Sunday as well as New Year's Day, they had a leisurely breakfast and attended a memorable service at St. Paul's Cathedral. The organ and the choir were outstanding. After services, Georgina and Basil informed Amy that they had invited two other couples to join them for dinner that day.

The guests arrived at two o'clock and drinks were served in the living room. Since it was a cold wet day, they had a crackling, warm fire blazing in the fireplace.

The door chimes sounded once again and Basil opened the door to welcome a smiling James Carstairs.

"Hello there, James. Happy New Year!" Greeting their guest with a hearty handshake, Basil added: "We're so glad you had no other plans for today so you could join our party."

"Thank you, Basil. I have been looking forward to it. Happy New Year. And here is Georgina." He gave her a hug.

"And here is Amy," said Georgina. "I'll bet that you're surprised to see her here."

He replied with a laugh: "Probably not half as surprised as she is to see me".

They all laughed at that, including Amy, who was indeed dumbfounded. He seemed to know everyone quite well, all of the men being lawyers. They sat down to dinner half an hour later with James and Amy sitting beside each other. His eyes twinkled as he whispered to Amy: "Do you think there is a conspiracy afoot?"

She whispered back: "I'm beginning to think so".

Georgina's cook had outdone herself with a delicious hot soup, followed by roast beef, popovers and a tasty tossed salad. To crown it all, Georgina had personally made a delicious trifle from an old family recipe. There were toasts again to the New Year and good health and fortune to all.

15

When the office re-opened after the holidays, James mentioned to Amy that he had enjoyed being with his sister Genevieve and her husband Ian for Christmas, but that a few days was more than enough.

"She is two years older than I am and as a youngster, she was the bane of my existence. For example, one day when we were fishing together, our lines got tangled up, she threw the can of worms at me and I still have a scar on my ankle to remind me where it cut me."

Amy laughed heartily at this.

She told him about how she enjoyed her time with Barbara and the family, and they settled down to work.

About two weeks later, James asked Amy to come to a musical with him—a lawyer friend was ill and had given him his two tickets. Since Amy loved musicals, she didn't even hesitate in saying yes.

They had wonderful box seats and enjoyed their evening together, even though Amy accidentally dropped her program down from the balcony. Both of them had a good chuckle over this, although Amy could not help but feel embarrassed.

Since the theatre time was early, James had asked her to go out for dinner afterwards. They seemed to be more comfortable in each other's company, and had many laughs over seemingly insignificant things.

He mentioned the painting again and told her that the art dealer had done some additional research on the artist. He had lived in the south of France, working in various artist colonies. He had died at sixty-one, and there were a few of his paintings in the collections of individuals and galleries right here in London. The dealer was attempting to assemble a group of paintings from area collectors and was planning a public showing.

"We must go together to see it," he said with a smile. "I guess we didn't discover him first, but I would like to see his other work."

"Oh yes," answered Amy, carefully remembering to put her napkin on the table. James noticed this and gave her a quick smile.

Late January was gloomy and rainy. It didn't help that their work load in the office was very heavy. One day, Amy got caught in a deluge on her way home. She was cold and wet. Despite a hot bath and some warm soup, Amy woke the next morning with a sore throat and a slight fever.

She decided that since it was Friday, she would finish the week at work. After arriving, James took one look at her red nose and irritated eyes and laughed: "Now where is my lovely secretary? I am sending you home in a taxi along with your germs. Please don't come back until you feel better."

After picking up some throat gargle, cough drops, chest rub and a few groceries, she arrived at her flat. Mrs. Fillmore saw her and said: "Now what has happened? You're back early."

Amy tried to answer but Mrs. Fillmore, noting her predicament said: "Now take two aspirins and get directly into bed, dear. I'll bring up some of my good chicken soup at lunchtime. It is very good for you. Oh, you poor dear."

Amy suffered with a runny nose, coughing and watery eyes for three days. Finally, on Monday, when she still seemed feverish and was starting to cough more, Barbara took her to the doctor's. He put her on antibiotics, which quickly brought her malady under control.

On Thursday, she felt well enough to return to work. James was very glad to see her, but he said in a gruff voice: "Well, I am so glad you're finally back. These temporary girls do not know how to spell or even type a letter properly, and worst of all I missed my lunch one day and at two o'clock had to order it myself. There is a pile of letters on your desk that will have to be re-done this morning."

Amy was a bit hurt and bewildered by his outburst and replied with a touch of impatience in her own voice: "I'm sorry to have been away so long. I will start the letters right away, sir."

He went into his office and closed the door. By one o'clock, she had heard nothing from him, so she ordered an extra nice lunch with all his favourites. She tapped on the door and he looked up saying: "Lunch time, already? Now this is what I have missed, my dear Amy taking care of me."

A few minutes later, a beautiful vase of flowers, her favourite, pink roses, was delivered to her desk. The card was signed: "Sorry. Sincerely, James."

He opened the door just as she had finished reading the card and was sniffing the sweet roses.

"I realize that I must have offended you by my coarse greeting. Please forgive this grumpy old bear. I really did miss you so. I hope you're feeling better, Amy."

Amy's eyes filled with tears. She had been offended; it wasn't her fault that she had caught that nasty cold. How sweet he was to apologize. So she said instead: "You didn't have to do this, but thank you so much. I love pink roses."

He patted her on the shoulder saying: "Now tell me that I am forgiven," noting those overly bright blue eyes. "You make me so comfortable. I don't like it when you're not here."

"It's nothing," she replied, really wanting to weep. I guess I'm still weak after my cold, she thought to herself. Aloud, she said: "Thank you, again."

James said: "So now let's be friends and get back to work. Please come in and take some dictation," he said with a smile.

That evening, Amy had invited Barbara to go to the symphony with her, using the tickets from James, and they both enjoyed it tremendously.

In late February, the Lebrandt collection had been assembled and James invited Amy to accompany him to the exhibition and to go out for dinner afterwards. They were both very excited and anxious to see other paintings that "their" artist had done.

When they arrived, James was greeted by the gallery owner who personally conducted them to the special section where A.A. Lebrandt's paintings were hung. The owner was very interested to hear that Amy also had a Lebrandt painting and asked if he might see it some time. James and Amy took their time looking at the art, deciding which other paintings they liked and finally concluding that their own pictures were the best.

Over dinner, they had more discussion about Lebrandt's work and some of the landscapes from other artists. They found that they liked many of the same artists and mutually disliked modern art. As they parted, they agreed that it had been a most exciting evening.

Work was hectic again and she felt like scolding James for overextending himself. There were many days when she had to order his lunch and make him take time to eat it. She was finding it a strain now and then to stay until five-thirty to do her extra work.

One Saturday, she made an appointment to have her hair and nails done at Giorgio's Salon and that helped a bit. She also went to Madame Zolie's and ordered a lovely grey tweed suit (very practical she thought) and a soft silk blouse to go with it. Between work and her social life, she seemed to need more outfits now.

She tried to see the grandchildren often, and even took them to the cinema and brought them back to her flat for tea afterwards. Of course, she had to serve fish-and-chips and soft drinks and she had made a lovely sponge cake for dessert.

They told her about school, and George said he had taken her advice about just going one day at a time. He was working a little harder on his homework and had even raised his grades to an excellent level. Stephanie said she was working harder too because she definitely wanted to become a nurse.

They also said that their parents had mentioned flying to Paris for a week this summer during the holidays. George thought the idea of an airplane flight much more exciting than anything else.

Amy went to their house for dinner the next Sunday to celebrate George's thirteenth birthday. They had his favourite dinner of roast beef with Yorkshire pudding and a lovely chocolate cake with thirteen candles on it.

"Call the fire department!" joked Jeffery, as George made a wish and blew out the candles. Amy gave him a radio, since she knew boys did not appreciate clothes. His parents did give him clothes as well as a sports bag, and Stephanie gave him a book about sports. He thanked everyone and gave each a hug.

"Thank goodness you're not too old yet to give hugs," said Amy lovingly.

"I never will be for you, Grandmother," said George. "Maybe Stephanie though." His sister gave him a punch despite it being his birthday.

Amy answered the phone one morning, the caller asking for Mr. Carstairs. When she tried to find out the name of the caller, the person hung up. About an hour later, the same person called again and got very agitated when Amy would not put the call through.

Amy told James about it and he reacted immediately saying: "I'm working on a case right now for a troubled young man. Perhaps it is his sister who keeps calling. I have heard that she is upset about the way I'm handling this case, but I'm doing what her brother wants."

At noon, James went out for lunch with a client. Amy sat at her desk typing and eating her sandwich. Suddenly, the door burst open and in came this lady, bristling with suppressed rage demanding: "Where is Mr. Carstairs? I must see Mr. Carstairs!"

"I am sorry. He is out for lunch right now," replied Amy. "Perhaps you would like to make an appointment and return later this afternoon."

With that, the woman seemed to lose control and pushed Amy back against her chair. Amy fell to the floor hitting her head on the desk. The woman then shoved open Mr. Carstairs' door, looking all around his office.

"I know you're here," she yelled. "You just don't want to see me or talk to me!"

Another partner heard what was happening and called security. He and another burly lawyer blocked the intruder's way.

"Out of my way," she yelled. A big security officer grappled with her. Two policemen arrived and soon had her under control.

Meanwhile, Amy was moaning on the floor and all attention was immediately focused on her. Just then, James came in. He rushed to her side and, putting an arm under her shoulders, said in a frightened voice: "My dear Amy, are you going to be all right? What has happened? Look at the bump on your forehead. Someone call an ambulance."

"Now please James, don't fuss so," she said. "I'm quite sure there is nothing wrong with me. Just help me to get up and sit in my chair."

"Let's get her a cup of tea, then," he motioned to one of the secretaries. "Also a cold cloth for her forehead would help," he ordered, finally getting himself under control, and sitting her down carefully in her chair.

Amy tried to tell him what had happened. "I should have made you lock the door during lunch hour, Amy," he said. "That woman should be locked up. I will speak to the police. This estate matter has become very complex and I really don't like the man or his sister. I will deal with them later. Here, drink your tea and keep this cold cloth on your head."

James made her sit and relax for at least half an hour, until he was certain that nothing was wrong. He then insisted on calling a taxi and sending her home.

"Put your feet up and have a rest," he ordered. "You will feel much better tomorrow."

Even though Amy still had a purple bruise on her forehead

and a couple of others elsewhere, she insisted on working the next day. She laughed heartily when James appeared at the office door at noon with a lovely light lunch for two. “It’s the least I can do for a heroine,” he said with a bow.

“You are a funny, dear man, James,” said Amy with a smile.

16

During the following week, the art dealer called to ask if he could take James and Amy out for dinner. They arranged to go to James's first for drinks to see his painting, then out to dinner, and finally to Amy's flat.

The dealer seemed to be in ecstasy over the two paintings and was fascinated to hear how and where each painting had been purchased. The evening was very interesting, with the dealer filling them in with the details of the artist's background. Amy and James were both pleased and flattered by his praise for their paintings.

Spring was approaching and Amy had been invited once again to her friends the Langfords for the weekend. They were to have dinner with Sir John and Lady Beaton on the Saturday night.

Amy packed carefully, wondering what to take, and left on Saturday morning on the ten-fifteen train. Doctor Jim and Vivian were both there at the Ferndene station to greet her with hugs and kisses.

"You look so like a Londoner now," said Vivian with a smile.

"Is that good or bad?" Amy enquired with a laugh.

"Oh, definitely very good."

It was so nice to look around the green countryside and to see daffodils nodding here and there. A loud voice in her ear made her jump, and there was Mrs. Epsom-Smythe. She had on an apple-green pantsuit with a blue and green scarf twisted around her neck.

"Here for another visit are you, Amy? It must be nice to escape from that nasty London air. It goes right to my lungs, isn't that so, Doctor? Well, I must find my daughter, Deidre, who is arriving for a visit also. Goodbye." And with that she sailed away down the platform.

Over a light lunch, they talked about all that had happened since Amy had last seen her friends. She learned that there had been an epidemic of chicken pox in Ferndene earlier that spring and even Jane's twins had not escaped it.

"Not too many missed it," stated Doctor Jim. "You can't help it with school-age children who pass it on to their brothers and sisters."

They took a walk around the garden admiring the spring flowers, which were Vivian's pride and joy. It was so peaceful here in Ferndene and Amy thought with sadness in her heart about what she had given up. In about a year, I will be finished working, she thought to herself.

Soon it was time to dress for dinner. She had mixed feelings again about seeing her house with someone else living in it.

They arrived promptly at six-thirty and were greeted first by Tilly, with a big hug for Amy. Lady Jane Beaton came forward, greeting her guests enthusiastically. She led them into the living room where Sir John was talking to another guest who had his back turned to them. He looked very familiar to Amy. He turned and they each looked with surprise and then big smiles lit up their faces.

"Amy"—"James"—they both exclaimed at the same time.

"I never suspected that you might be included in tonight's festivities," said Amy.

"I hesitated to tell you that I was going to be a guest in your house in case it would disturb you," said James gently. "I hope that you will forgive me, my dear."

"No, no," she stammered. "I mean yes. I'm very glad to see you".

"Now I must tell you how very comfortable we have become in your home, dear Amy," said Lady Jane. "James has been telling me how very much he absolutely adores it too, have you not, James?"

"Oh yes," he said. "I don't know how you can bear to live in London after owning this beautiful home."

"My grandparents and then my parents lived here and I inherited it from them. They had very good taste, so the house came to me pretty well as you see it. Of course, it was difficult to leave it, but your sales pitch was irresistible, and I have the comfort of knowing that I will be returning here within a year and a bit."

They chatted amiably and enjoyed a cocktail (not sherry) and then went in to dinner. Amy was placed beside James. Tilly served and occasionally her niece came out too as she was catering the meal.

Conversation was very humorous, Sir John having some wonderful stories to tell about his days in the diplomatic service. They especially liked the one about an elephant stampede that trampled through their compound. The doctor talked about some of his demanding patients, young and old, and James related some tales of adventure when he was younger and had travelled to Switzerland. Everyone got along very well indeed.

Over coffee, James apologized again for not telling Amy that he would be visiting her home, but she made light of it all, repeating that she was so pleased that he liked Bower House. Secretly, James was wondering now just what had prompted Amy to lease her house and take the job, and rapidly reached his own conclusion.

Amy went to the kitchen to see Tilly again before she left.

"Your boss is a wonderful man, Amy. You must enjoy working for him."

"I do," replied Amy, as she gave Tilly a final hug.

Amy, Vivian and Jim said their thank yous and goodbyes to their hosts. When they got home, Amy remarked: "I was so surprised to see James Carstairs there. I had no idea he was coming to Ferndene for the weekend. He thought I might be upset about the idea of him being at my house but I wasn't, just surprised."

Jim and Vivian thought it a great joke.

Spring had fully arrived and even London was alive with greenery. Many window boxes sported lovely flowers. The parks were crowded with people strolling and admiring the beauty of the gardens around them.

Mrs. Fillmore had a small garden at the back. She was proud of her box hedges and her tubs of flowers. There were two lovely dark green wrought iron benches face to face, with a small table between.

She invited Amy to have tea in the garden after dinner one night, and served her famous cake. Amy took a stroll around the garden with her as she talked about all the different plantings. Two lilac trees were in bud and Mrs. Fillmore told Amy that her husband had planted these in his more robust days.

Of course, spring rains were a part of all this and one just got used to carrying an umbrella about. The Chelsea Flower Show is a must-see event in May of each year, and Barbara, Georgina and Amy made a day of it. They left first thing in the morning on a Saturday. There was not too much of a crowd just after nine and they walked around admiring all the displays. By eleven-thirty, they decided to rest their weary feet and eyes and have an early lunch of sandwiches and tea.

"Just too much to take in at once," declared Georgina. "My little note pad is full already."

"It gives you so many ideas for your garden," said Amy.

"And for floral designs," added Barbara.

They only stayed until one-thirty, and then dragged themselves to the car, and home.

James and Amy kept working five days a week with hardly any breaks for the next while. They were simply overwhelmed with work. James was having a little stomach trouble and asked for some Alka-Seltzer with water. He went home one day complaining of a stomach ache. Amy was starting to worry about him and caught him a couple of times clutching and rubbing his stomach.

"Now, James, you really must see a doctor. I'm sure something is seriously wrong with you."

"Oh no," he answered, "it's just something I ate."

A couple of days later, he pressed the buzzer and she found him retching and gasping with his hand at his side and doubled over in pain. She grabbed a wastebasket and some tissue for him and said: “Now, I am calling an ambulance, James. Clearly, something is seriously wrong.” His face was grey and he was sweating profusely.

The attendants were soon there with a stretcher and, after speaking to James and Amy, put him on it and started to carry him off.

“Which hospital will he be in?” she asked.

They replied with the name of one that was nearby. She didn’t know what to do first but, calming herself down, she called his home number and told his butler what had happened and suggested that he immediately contact James’s sister.

She decided that she couldn’t stand not knowing what was happening, so she took a taxi to the hospital. After waiting a long half-hour, the nurse came out and told her that James was having an operation to remove his appendix. Amy decided she would stay until the operation was over and she had heard from the doctor about his condition. She explained to the nurse that she was his personal secretary and since his sister lived out of town, she would not arrive for a while.

Amy drank two cups of tea, and paced the hall for two hours, until a doctor came out to speak to her.

“We managed to remove the appendix before it burst, thankfully. He’ll be fine in a few days, but he’ll have to stay here. Had he been having some trouble with his stomach lately?”

“Yes,” she answered, “but the attack today was very bad. I’ve been worried about him.”

“Well, after a few days in our hands, he will gradually get his strength back. Your quick action pretty well saved his life, you know. You told the nurse he has a sister?”

“Yes,” she said. “I’m sure she will be here soon. Thank you, doctor.”

Since hospital rules prevented her from seeing James as he was still in recovery, she felt she could go home. Amy decided to take a taxi, being too spent to go back to the office.

The following day, she went into the office to straighten up some papers and answer phone calls. At about four o'clock, she left work early and decided to go to the hospital to see how James was doing. He looked rather pale and weak, and was hooked up to a couple of drips, but he still could smile at her.

"Thank you, my guardian angel," he said. "The doctor thinks you saved my life."

Amy answered: "I'm so glad I was there when you needed me. Now, maybe you'll get some rest. I just wanted to make sure you were coming along all right today."

He motioned to the beautiful bouquet of flowers sitting on a nearby table. "From the staff, it says. Are you included in that?"

"Yes indeed," she replied. "We all wish you well. I mustn't stay too long. By the way, did your sister arrive yesterday?"

"Yes she did, and she was in earlier this afternoon. Thank you for telling her about my illness."

"Can I take care of anything at the office for you?"

"Just finish typing up the letters and perhaps go in mornings until I return, which should be in a week."

"Please call if you need anything," she said. "I'm so glad you're getting better. Goodbye, James."

She found herself worrying when he didn't call the next day, so she went to visit him again. She brought him two papers to sign, and a newspaper and two magazines to read.

"Thank you for your concern," he said with a weak smile. "I am feeling much better and should be out of the hospital in two or three more days."

In fact, James returned to the office in a week, and brought her a lovely box of chocolates as a token of his gratitude.

"Thank you again, dear Amy, for your care."

He promised to take it easy that week, so he went home at four o'clock every day. His colour gradually returned and he was soon back to his old self.

"I have been given another pair of tickets to the ballet by my old friend who is still ill. Would you like to go with me on Saturday night?" he asked.

"That would be delightful," she answered with a smile.

He promised to pick her up at seven-thirty. She fussed over what she would wear and decided to wear a soft satin blouse under her velvet suit. It was the perfect time of year to wear it. She washed her hair and set it in soft waves around her head.

Now what on earth is the matter with me? I feel like I'm getting ready for a date like when in my teens. The truth hit her—she enjoyed James's company very much.

"This old friend of yours is taking his time getting better," she remarked with some suspicion.

"Oh, I also forgot to mention that he gave me tickets to the theatre in three weeks. It's for that wonderful new musical that's so popular. These tickets are very hard to get."

"You do make it difficult for me to say no," she laughed.

"It's a date then?" he asked, with a twinkle in his eye.

"Of course, and thank you."

Basil and Georgina had asked her out for dinner the following Saturday. They were celebrating Basil's birthday. Amy gave him a bottle of French wine—a label that brought back so many memories of their idyllic vacation. Basil was very appreciative of this thoughtful gift.

On Sunday, it was Stephanie's twelfth birthday. She had twelve girl friends to the house for a party on Saturday, since she was a popular young girl and had trouble making up her list. Amy had some difficulty shopping for her gift, but ended up buying her a clock radio. Stephanie was always last out of bed.

Jeffery picked Amy up and she was greeted with much affection as she said "Happy Birthday" to Stephanie.

"How was your party yesterday, dear?" asked Amy.

"I had a wonderful time. Mother had made sandwiches for us, and we had ice cream, cake and punch. I got some great presents. Look at the decorations."

For dinner, there was stuffed chicken and another cake. Stephanie loved her radio and thanked Amy sincerely.

"Imagine, two birthday parties for me."

On Tuesday, a red-haired, blue-eyed middle-aged woman, came into the office.

"How do you do," she said with a smile. "I am James's sister. You must be the Mrs. Somerset that James talks of constantly. According to him, you are the very best secretary he has ever had."

"Far from perfect, believe me," Amy replied.

Just then, James, hearing his sister, came out and introduced them. "This is my sister, Genevieve Fleming, Amy."

"I'm trying to wrangle an invitation to lunch, James," said Genevieve. "I hope you can spare some time. I'm just in town for the day."

"Well, it will have to be quick," he replied. "I have a one-thirty appointment. Let's go right now."

Genevieve nodded and smiled at Amy saying: "I enjoyed meeting you and thank you for saving James's life."

Over lunch, Genevieve teased James about his competent secretary and was quite surprised when at one point, he snapped at her: "She is a very good secretary, Genevieve. I enjoy her company. Now let's change the subject."

Genevieve reported this incident to her husband that evening, setting off speculation about James's intentions towards Amy. Little did they realize that his intentions were becoming very serious. He was coming to know and love his brave, efficient secretary who had been through so much and was trying to cope with her finances by returning to work and leasing her beautiful house

How much the loss of her husband still affected her, James did not know. It had been eighteen months since William had died. James was afraid to advance too quickly with their relationship, but he couldn't help feeling and hoping that marriage would be the outcome. He thought they should just go on as they were—getting to know each other better.

Amy too, was examining her feelings. She only occasionally had time to think of William now, mainly because she was too busy working, and there was always something going on over the weekends. To be honest, her feelings for James were very profound. At work, it was easy to numb herself to these conflicting emotions. When they went out somewhere together however, she enjoyed his companionship, humour and intelligence very much. They had so much in common. She also decided just to enjoy their relationship as it was for now and to see what developed. It was too soon for anything more.

Mid-summer turned sultry. One Wednesday, James announced in the morning that he had decided to take the rest of the day off.

"I know this is very out of character for me," he joked, "but we have both been working too hard. I feel like having an adventure today. Would you like to drive out to Wisley Gardens with me and have lunch there? I know it seems to be a rather wicked idea, but I really need a break. We will be back in town by five."

Amy was a little hesitant at first, and really didn't know what to say.

"Please say yes," he pleaded. "I don't ordinarily take days off, as you know, but I have felt very harassed lately."

"Well, that would be lovely," she answered with a nod and a smile.

"Just walk nonchalantly by my side. My car is parked behind the building in the car park."

When they got in the car, James started to laugh and then Amy did too.

"I feel like a truant from school," he joked. He manoeuvred the car through the traffic and out onto the Motorway. Within an hour, they were at Wisley Gardens. Since it was fairly early, there weren't too many people about.

They walked through the wrought iron gates, past the Laboratory, which overlooked a formal canal strewn with water lilies. On one side was a broad border backed by shrubs, with English roses and perennials. They went on to the Formal Garden, laid out as a parterre. It presented a rainbow of colour.

"How marvellous!" remarked Amy.

Then came the Portsmouth Field, which at this time of summer featured different cultivars of delphinium and sweet peas. They decided this was one of their favourite sights.

After almost two hours, they were very warm, footsore and

thirsty. James and Amy found the Conservatory Café and ate a light lunch, with two glasses of lemonade each to quench their thirst.

They strolled through two more areas of these extensive gardens. At three-thirty, James suggested that they should head home to London. As he dropped her off at her flat, they thanked each other for a very enjoyable day.

17

The next morning started off with James dictating about a dozen letters which she typed, and also many phone calls which she put through to him.

By one o'clock, she had eaten her sandwich but he had not had his lunch. She ordered one of his favourite sandwiches and, adding some tea and biscuits, put everything on a tray, knocked on his door, and went in.

"How good of you to think of me," he said with a smile. "I got so caught up in the letters I was reading. You typed them perfectly as usual."

She put the tray down on the corner of the desk and put the plate with his sandwich and biscuits near him. As she went to pour his tea, she bumped the corner of the desk, spilling tea on his coat sleeve and on the letter which he had been reading.

He jumped back clear of any more tea and they each grabbed handkerchiefs and tissues to soak up the spill.

"Oh, I am so sorry," she gasped with tears starting in her eyes. "Look at your jacket and the freshly-typed letter. Let me take your jacket and run down to the dry cleaners with it," she said, getting behind him and helping to take it off, hoping he had not seen her tears. It was too late, he had seen them and his inclination was to comfort her on his shoulder. Instead, he patted her on the shoulder and said: "My dear Amy, my shirtsleeves are not even wet, and I am sure the dry cleaners will have no problem at all in cleaning the coat by four o'clock. I will eat my lunch and have the rest of the tea while you're gone. The letter is no loss; you can reprint it from the computer."

"Oh yes," she said, trying to smile. "I'll be back in a few minutes. Again, I am sorry."

"Now, not one more word about it."

The letter was later reprinted and signed without further ado.

She went down to the dry cleaners at four and returned with James's jacket. It looked like new. "Now we'll keep this a little secret of our own," he said with a laugh.

Four more letters had to be sent out, so it was five-thirty before they were done.

"I don't suppose you would consider coming to that nice café again for a steak and kidney pie for dinner would you? I have no one at home to make my dinner tonight, so I would either make an egg and toast or starve. I am not a very good cook."

He had such a pleading look on his face, that Amy laughed out loud and said: "Now how can I resist a starving man? Let's go."

"Thank you," he replied.

Over dinner, they talked again about the enjoyable time they had at the gardens and how the spontaneity of the outing had made it all the more enjoyable.

"I must play truant more often," he said seriously. "I work too hard. Thanks for coming to dinner with me."

Barbara and Jeffery had decided to have a little dinner party on the Sunday. They invited James and Amy as well as Basil and Georgina. Barbara was wondering exactly what was going on between her mother and James Carstairs. She seemed to be seeing a lot of him outside the office. Were things getting serious? She talked this over with Jeffery, who told her to let things slide for a while; Amy was a grown woman and knew what she was doing. "James is a well-respected lawyer and an honourable man. The two of them seem to get along very well, that's all."

Sunday was a glorious day and James called Amy early to ask if she would mind if he came to service with her. He picked her up and they both enjoyed hearing the clear voices and the inspiring sermon.

Amy had worn her lovely, pale blue summer dress since it was so warm. James told her how becoming it was. He gave her one of his winsome, soft smiles that made her heart do a flip-flop, as he held the car door for her.

Everyone seemed to be out in the parks trying to get the most enjoyment out of the beautiful weather.

"I don't believe you have seen my little garden at the back of my townhouse," mentioned James. "You must come and see it one day. I like to putter around it when I have time, but mostly a gardener comes in once a week to do the heavy work."

"I suppose you saw the garden at my home in Ferndene?" she asked. "My grandparents and parents started it all, and William put in the circular rose garden. I guess I've always had a love for flowers. When Barbara was growing up I started to take botanical drawing lessons. William always seemed to be working, so I had plenty of time on my hands. I grew to love the work, especially using watercolours to tint the drawings and went into some local art shows. I was lucky enough to sell a few paintings and this paid for more lessons and painting equipment."

"My dear Amy!" said James in an admiring voice. "How you do keep surprising me. All these hidden talents. I would love to see some of your work."

"Well," she answered matter-of-factly, "Barbara has a few pieces and I have hung a couple in my flat. It was fun to go into competitions and I also did a few illustrations for a book."

"Now you must show me some of your work today at Barbara's," he said as they pulled into their driveway. Barbara and Jeffery greeted them at the door as they arrived for the dinner party. Two minutes later, Georgina and Basil arrived too.

"Please come in everyone," said Jeffery.

"We're going to have cocktails on the patio first," announced Barbara, as she led them out through the lovely French doors. The patio was made of flagstone and also had a wall of stone. At intervals were cement pots filled with mixed plantings of flowers and ivy.

Everyone ended up having sherry except Amy, of course, who had a light gin with lots of tonic and lemon.

"We all know that sherry goes right to your head, Amy," said James, and everyone laughed including Amy herself. They talked about the weather and enquired whether anyone had plans for a summer holiday. Basil and Georgina were going to Rome for a week, and Barbara and Jeffery were taking the children to Paris for a week. They had tried to get Amy to go with them, but she said that when her vacation time came, she would visit in Ferndene for a couple of days and otherwise stay in town. James mentioned visiting his sister in September, so perhaps Amy would take her time off then too.

Dinner was announced shortly and everyone filed into the

dining room. James and Amy sat beside each other. A cold potato and leek soup started the meal. A delicious filet of sole was served next with crisp vegetables. Georgina and Basil complimented Barbara, and also commented on the wonderful food they were served on their holiday in France with Amy last year.

Barbara said that they were looking forward to wonderful meals in Paris. Jeffery added that he and their son George had great appetites and would eat anything and lots of it. Everyone laughed at this.

James lamented that he was such a terrible cook and that he ate out if there was no one there to cook for him. In fact, he and Amy had worked late on Wednesday and had eaten at the café around the corner. "They have the most delicious steak and kidney pie," he added.

"Yes," laughed Amy. "As a matter of fact, even Tilly can't make it any better, but please don't tell her."

After dinner, James mentioned that he had just found out about Amy's talent for botanical drawing. He asked Barbara if she would mind showing him some of Amy's work.

Of course, they all wanted to see them. Amy felt embarrassed, but Barbara said: "She's too modest; I will be happy to show them to you. We have six of them. Mother sold quite a few you know and won several prizes too."

Amy and Jeffery stayed on the patio as the others went around the different rooms looking at her paintings.

Georgina came back saying: "Now Amy, you must get back to your art. You could pick up a Saturday morning class or an evening class to refresh your drawing. I had forgotten how wonderful they are. Why didn't I get more than one?"

James returned and said with much admiration: "My dear Amy, they are wonderful indeed—so life-like and the colours are superb. Now I'm worried that you will desert me as a secretary and become a famous artist," he added with a laugh and a glow in his eyes that was not lost on anyone.

Amy, much embarrassed, with pink cheeks, smiled and said: "I don't think I would ever do that, James. My art has always been just a sideline, but perhaps I could be tempted to make it a full-time career."

Before the party broke up, Stephanie and George came in the door in high spirits. They greeted Grandmother with a hug and kiss and shook hands politely with everyone.

They reported that they had been to a birthday party at their cousin's and had a famous time.

James and Amy said thank you and goodbye to Barbara and Jeffery, as did Georgina and Basil. James drove Amy back to her flat saying that he liked Barbara and her family very much and that Amy had done a fine job raising her daughter. "Your grandchildren are lovely children. I can see that they certainly love their grandmother."

That night Barbara said to Jeffery: "Did you see that glance between Mother and James? I tell you this is getting serious."

Georgina and Basil were having the same conversation about James and Amy.

18

Jeffery and Barbara left for Paris with the children in the third week of August. Amy had been told by the children at one of their Sunday dinners together that the best part of the vacation was going to be the plane trip.

"Father has been rehearsing some French with us at dinner for the past two weeks. I don't want to starve there," exclaimed George. "I've learned to say pommes frites, le boeuf, l'omelet and chocolat—important things like that."

"Please plan to come for tea on the Sunday after our return, Mother," said Barbara. "It's your birthday and in addition I'm sure the children won't rest until they've told you every detail of their trip."

"We'll send you a postcard, Grandmother. Au revoir," giggled Stephanie.

Amy was extra busy at work that week, and James had invited her for a concert and dinner on Saturday night.

"More tickets from your friend?" she asked with a grin.

"Not this time, my dear Amy. I bought them myself," he answered with a twinkling smile.

She had made an appointment with Giorgio the hairdresser for Saturday morning, and decided to have a manicure too. 'It will be nice to spoil myself.'

The concert was a sell-out and the orchestra played many lovely operetta pieces. As they walked around during intermission, she and James met several acquaintances, and he guided her skillfully through the crowd by lightly tucking his hand into the crook of her arm.

The chimes sounded and they took their seats again, the music making them feel very light-hearted. After the performance, they taxied to a restaurant, which they had enjoyed before. As soon as they were seated, Amy started to giggle.

"What is it, Amy?"

"Do you realize that I once dropped my serviette in front of you in this very restaurant?"

"And I, thinking you were flirting with me, picked it up, ready to serve the beautiful Mrs. Somerset."

With feigned indignation on her face, she replied: "I was not flirting, as you say. It was a genuine accident, Mr. Carstairs."

With that, he raised her hand to his lips.

She withdrew her hand in a fluster and said: "Now what do you fancy for dinner tonight, James?" trying to ignore his smiling gaze.

"I'm sorry to tease you like that," he said.

She started to laugh and then so did he.

"Anything but the scallops," he replied. "They never agree with me, so I'm going to order a medium filet."

"I'm going to have a filet too," she said, and added: "I don't like broccoli. I was in the hospital for ten days a few years ago when I had a rather major surgery and they served nothing but over-cooked broccoli as a vegetable." He laughed as she added: "I have never eaten it since."

"Do you realize there are still many things that we don't know about each other, not major things, but minor little things?"

As they ate their delicious filets, baked potato and salad, James added that he never ate parsnips, but he particularly disliked inefficient secretaries.

"Now, let's see if there are other things I can tell you, James—I can't stand to have wilted or dead flowers in the house, and I hate untidiness; also, I don't like Brussels sprouts." Again, they laughed in unison.

"Now, I'm hearing about the real Amy."

"I was going to settle a holiday time for a week in late September. I hope that Friday, the twenty-second will suit you, Amy. Also, my sister and her husband are coming up to London a week from Wednesday just for an overnight stay, and they want us to join them for dinner that evening. She wants another opportunity to express her gratitude to you for sending me off to hospital on time last spring."

Amy replied: "Of course, I'd love to see Genevieve again and to meet her husband, but she shouldn't feel that any debt is owed."

"Now don't worry," he said. "Genevieve is just showing you a gesture of friendship and thanks."

"Well, I guess that will be fine then," she answered, concerned perhaps that his family would be looking her over.

"As to the twenty-second of September for a vacation, that sounds great. Vivian Langford and her husband have been after me to visit them again, and I hope to see my house again. Also,

I want some time in the city to just relax, go out for lunch with Barbara and Georgina, and do some shopping."

"I've been invited to Genevieve's for a couple of days, and also to play golf with a friend. My plans are easy too," replied James. "I think we both need time away from work, and some fresh air."

After dinner, James found a taxi. As he dropped her off at her flat, he smiled and said: "I enjoyed our evening together very much, my dear. Good night."

She thanked him and added that she also had a good time.

On the Sunday after their return from France, Jeffery picked Amy up at two o'clock to bring her back to their house for tea.

"How was your trip to Paris, Jeffery?" she asked as she got into the car.

"We had a lovely time together, but it's quite different having two children along. They seem to dominate the activities of the day, but they were very good sports about it all. We had best wait and let the children tell you what we did."

As they came into the house, everyone shouted "Happy Birthday" to Amy. George and Stephanie both gave her a big hug and kiss, saying they were so glad she had come. She was very pleased by this noisy welcome.

Barbara gave Amy a hug and kiss too, and said how glad they were to share her birthday with her. The children pulled her into the living room and sat her in a comfortable wing chair.

"Now Grandmother, just listen as we tell you all about Paris," said George. "We went to the top of the Eiffel Tower the first day, and had pommes frites on a bench afterwards."

"Next," interrupted Stephanie, "we went to the Louvre, only

because we had to, but I guess it was good for us to see things like Winged Victory and the Mona Lisa and a lot of other things there."

"It took so long we only had time to go back to the hotel and change and rest for a few minutes before we went out for dinner," said George. "The restaurant had a tented ceiling in black and white stripes and was very posh. I read the menu carefully to see if there was anything decent to eat on it. Remember, Father had been working on our practical French." Proudly he added: "I ordered le boeuf and une salade on the side. Now the desserts were top notch and I remembered you telling me about the Gateau St. Honoré that you had in southern France, so that's what I ordered for dessert."

Everyone laughed over this recital, even George himself.

"And what did you have on your first night, Stephanie?" asked Amy.

"Well, I stuck to the things I knew. I ordered le poulet à l'orange and une salade, like George. Also, the same dessert. It sure was scrumptious. Mother and Father ordered escargots, which were the most disgusting things I've ever seen. Imagine eating snails! You see them in the garden, for goodness sake!"

The adults all laughed until it hurt.

"We had fresh-baked croissants and jam every morning," added George. "They were great!"

"What else did you do besides eat, my dears?" asked Amy.

"We enjoyed a sight-seeing boat down the Seine River at night so much," said Stephanie, "that we begged to do it again during the day just to see all those beautiful bridges."

"We split up one day. While the girls looked at the fancy shops, George and I went on the Métro—the underground train. It's much the same as ours, we found, only quite lavish and more modern," added Jeffery.

"We found the shops were much too expensive for one thing, except some antique shops," said Barbara, "but we discovered a nice little café for lunch."

Stephanie piped up with: "We went to see Versailles outside Paris, a most gorgeous palace. King Louis the Fourteenth built it, you know. We saw the Hall of Mirrors and the lovely gardens. But my favourite was the Petit Trianon which was Marie Antoinette's hide-away. We were so tired that night that we ordered up room service."

"Well you certainly seem to have had a great time, but you didn't tell me about your flight," said Amy.

Stephanie said: "We loved it, but when it got a bit bumpy, George had to get out the air sickness bag."

George went to get up and give her a poke, but a stern glance from his father made him sit down. Barbara intervened with: "Now let's have our tea, shall we? Stephanie bring out the present that we brought home for Grandmother."

Stephanie came forward with a nicely wrapped birthday present for Amy. She opened it, and there was a pair of lovely earrings, three pearls nestled together in each.

"Why, how sweet," she said. "Now there you go again, making me want to cry. You are so thoughtful. I expected that it would be a miniature Eiffel Tower."

George laughed uproariously at this, saying that he and Stephanie had each bought one for themselves as a souvenir.

A generous tea was served along with a birthday cake for Amy. They sang Happy Birthday and wished her well once more. Barbara asked her mother what she had been doing while they were away.

Amy replied: "Well, I worked hard all week, and then James took me to a concert and dinner on Saturday night. We had a wonderful time. His sister and her husband are going to be in town this week and want to take James and me out for dinner. James says that she wants to thank me again for what he terms 'saving his life' by getting him to the hospital last spring when he took sick. I've only met her once for a few minutes but she did write a lovely note afterwards. Barbara, I somehow feel I'm up for inspection and I'm quite nervous about this dinner."

"Now don't be silly, Mother. Just be your loveable self. She just wants to get to know you better."

"Well, I can't help it. James has tried to reassure me too, but I still have reservations. I should head home now. I've enjoyed visiting very much, and it sounds like you had a wonderful time. You are naughty to have brought home such an extravagant present for me, but I love the earrings."

With hugs and kisses all around, she said goodbye and Jeffery drove her home once again. She was quite full after such a large tea so she just had toast and tea for dinner.

Amy searched through her wardrobe trying to decide on what to wear to Wednesday's dinner, and finally chose her pink suit with her new pearl earrings. She also got her office clothes ready for the next day. As she went to bed, she found herself reading over the same few pages in her book, and finally gave herself up to sleep.

When she arrived at the office on Monday, there was a box of chocolates with a large red ribbon resting on her desk. She opened the accompanying birthday card which was signed: "Love, James." Her heart skipped a beat when she read the card. As he was with a client, his door was closed and she did not have the opportunity to thank him until mid-morning.

Wednesday came all too soon. James and Amy quit work at

four o'clock to prepare for the evening. Since her clothes were decided on, she had a warm shower and washed her hair. The suit looked lovely, having been freshly cleaned, and she was so proud of her new pearl earrings. She carried a light beige purse and wore light beige pumps. She was at the door promptly at six when James pulled up in his car.

"My, my, you certainly look extra special tonight," he said. "What a becoming colour for you."

They arrived at the restaurant just in time to see Genevieve and her husband going in. As they were seated in the outer room, Genevieve introduced Amy to her husband, Ian, and James said in his charming way: "How thoughtful of you to get the four of us together tonight."

Amy picked up on his cue and said: "Yes, it's so nice to see you again, Genevieve, and I'm glad to meet you, Ian."

"We wanted to thank you again Amy for taking such good care of James last spring when he had to be hospitalized. Of course, he praises you to the skies so I felt we must get to know each other better. A note was not enough."

James gave Amy's hand a squeeze under the table. "Now Genevieve, don't embarrass Amy any further."

Her husband thought it wise to change the subject at this point and told them that he was in London on business and that Genevieve wanted a chance to shop.

"Yes, I've had a lovely time, but I must admit I'll be glad to get back to the peace and quiet of our country existence," she replied.

Just then, the headwaiter called them into the main part of the restaurant and led them to their table. James made sure that Amy was right beside him and tried to lead the conversation on a light course. They decided on their menu choices and then

Genevieve turned to Amy saying: "How do you like living in London again?"

"Well, I find I really do like living in the city. My husband, William, and I lived in London for over twenty-five years and we raised our daughter Barbara here. Now, I love the fact that I can see the grandchildren so often. Your brother is not too exacting as a boss, and we manage to get through most days without testing my rusty talents too badly.

"Thanks to James, I was able to lease my house in Ferndene to his friends the Beatons. I've seen the house on two occasions when visiting my old friends Vivian Langford and her husband, Doctor Jim. The Beatons are taking very good care of it. My long-time friend, Tilly, works for them, so things are going on much as before."

"I happened to be visiting the Beatons the very weekend that Amy was visiting the Langfords," James interjected. "Amy's home is truly beautiful and so is her garden. I also learned recently that Amy had done botanical drawings and watercolours for many years. They are quite good."

"How did you come to be a secretary, Amy?" asked Genevieve.

"Well, it's a rather long story. Georgina, my best friend in school, was Lady Brocklehurst's granddaughter. The Lady was my grandmother's best friend. Between the two of them, they decided that girls of that time should not be idle, going to parties and so on, but doing something useful like charity work or having a job. Lady Brocklehurst pretty well bullied us into taking a secretarial course, and then helped us to get our jobs at Carstairs and Carstairs.

"It was there that we both met our future husbands. I returned to work there after our daughter grew up and I continued until my husband suffered ill health. Unfortunately, after three years of retirement, he passed away."

James added: "Amy's grandfather was Colonel Thomas Teasdale and her father was the doctor in Ferndene."

"Well, you certainly have an interesting history, my dear," said Genevieve, much impressed.

"Yes, indeed," said Ian. "It's always fascinating to learn of one's background."

"Well, right now I'm enjoying working for James and I'm quite content with my life," Amy said with a smile.

The talk turned to gardens and James gave Amy a little wink, confirming that she had passed "the test." She smiled back at him. This did not pass unnoticed by Genevieve.

"So, are you coming down to see us two weeks from Saturday, James?"

"Yes, if that is fine with you," he replied.

"Would you like to play a game of golf, old boy?" Ian asked.

"I would love to," answered James. "I plan on visiting my friend Stuart Fenton, starting on the Monday, to play golf for three days. He has two other men joining us to make up a foursome. I don't know how well I will play. Golfing just four or five times a year doesn't make for good play, you know."

They all laughed.

Genevieve said to Amy: "Thank you again for taking good care of my brother. He also tells me that you order his luncheon when he forgets to eat. You are obviously a very valuable secretary."

After eating a delicious meal, they said goodbye to each other and prepared to leave.

"Thank you for the delightful dinner, Genevieve and Ian," Amy said with a smile, glad to be on amicable terms with James's family.

As they drove away, Amy let out a long sigh.

"Now what is that all about?" asked James, turning to look at her. "You were wonderful."

"I just felt as if I were under a microscope," replied Amy. "It was a somewhat uncomfortable evening."

"Now knowing my sister, you have jumped yards in her respect. She will think you're next to royalty," said James, trying to reassure her.

"James, you shouldn't have told her about my grandfather and father," Amy protested.

"Yes, I should," answered James. "Genevieve can be a bit of a snob sometimes and that is just what she needed to put her in her place." He patted her hand saying: "Now don't fret anymore about this evening. You are a wonderful, sweet woman, and you did very well tonight just as I expected you would. How about we do something by ourselves on Saturday night, and I get tickets to the ballet or symphony? There must be something playing in town that we would enjoy. Please let me make it up to you." He put on his pleading look.

"Oh James, you are so silly," she laughed. "I'm wondering if we are not seeing too much of each other. We also work together five days a week."

"I wouldn't mind if it were seven days a week," he answered, patting her hand again. "I enjoy every moment we spend together, my dear Amy."

As he looked into her eyes, Amy dropped her own in confusion and said: "Well, for now, I will see you at work tomorrow and yes, I would enjoy a quiet evening on Saturday."

James dropped her off at her flat, wondering if he should have declared himself at that point. Was she not ready for the serious talk he wanted? He was sure that she was enjoying his company. Were her thoughts turning to love too?

Amy went upstairs and shed a few tears, mostly relieving the tension of the evening. I know James is getting serious, she thought. It has been almost two years since William's death. I never thought I would re-marry until I slowly started to get to know James. Am I ready yet? What will Barbara think? Will she feel that I am being disloyal to her father's memory?

She shed a few more tears before she went to sleep, knowing full well that she had fallen in love with James.

She got up late the next morning, but thank goodness, after much hurrying, arrived at the office at the same time as James. The next two days were so busy that neither of them had further time for reflection.

19

James got tickets for the symphony on Saturday night as promised. They sat in companionable silence, listening to the familiar music. When James gently took Amy's hand in his, she did not pull away. During intermission, they talked about their favourite music. James mentioned the fact that his parents made him take the French horn for five years.

"They finally realized that I was not good at it and the music teacher told them he thought a sport activity was more my talent. At that point, my music career came to an end." Amy was very amused by his story.

She admitted that she had studied the piano for eight years, but could only play a few pieces well. She was certainly never destined to become a concert pianist.

"Well, as long as we can appreciate good music, that's what counts," he said with a smile.

Amy told him she was going to Georgina and Basil's for dinner the next day. "I haven't seen them for about three weeks. They went to Rome for a week's holiday. Basil is good with languages and speaks Italian fairly well, so I'm sure they got along just fine."

"I would love to go to Rome again," remarked James. "Perhaps, some day soon," he added with a twinkle in his eye. Amy didn't know what to think.

James dropped her off at her flat and said: "I will see you on Monday. Thank you for coming tonight, my dear."

"Thank you, James. Good night."

Dinner at Georgina's was a hilarious affair. Basil seemed to have an endless supply of stories about their Rome vacation that kept the girls in fits of laughter.

"I tried to call you last night," said Georgina. "Where were you?"

"Oh, James and I went to the symphony," Amy replied, trying to sound casual.

"How lovely," said Georgina, but her tone was questioning.

"I might as well tell you now that his sister and her husband were in town last Wednesday and they insisted on taking us out to dinner. They said that it was to thank me for taking care of James when he had to go to the hospital last spring. But, I tell you Georgina that I was a nervous wreck. James was very sweet, trying to keep the conversation free and easy, but I felt that I was being scrutinized for some reason."

"Excuse me, ladies," interrupted Basil. "I must spend a bit of time in my study to look up a few details concerning tomorrow's case." He saw that the ladies needed time for serious talk.

Tears sprang into Amy's eyes. Georgina tried to comfort her saying: "Things can't be that bad. Perhaps it will help you to talk things out. Now, first of all, if you don't know it already, all of your friends and family do. The obvious fact is that you're in love with one another. Only a goose wouldn't see that."

"But Georgina," Amy sniffed, "I don't know whether I'm ready for a permanent commitment. I somehow feel disloyal to William's memory, and wonder if it isn't too soon. What will Barbara think?"

"Now Amy, do you enjoy James's company?"

"Oh yes," she replied with feeling. "Somehow or other he always has some perfectly reasonable excuse for going out here or there. I can't resist saying 'yes' to these kind invitations. And we always have such enjoyable times."

"Has he had a serious talk with you about your relationship?"

"No-o-o, but I have a feeling that he has come close on several occasions. I always try to change the subject. I don't know what my answer will be."

"Do you love him?" Georgina asked bluntly.

"Yes, I must admit I do."

"Well then, let things go on a while longer and I have a feeling that when James senses that you're ready, he'll ask you to marry him. He's a wonderful man, Amy, and you're a delightful, brave woman. Just keep going."

"Our holidays are coming up soon, so we'll be apart for a whole week. That will give us both time to think," said Amy.

At that moment, Basil emerged from his study and offered to drive Amy home. When he returned, Georgina told him about her talk with Amy.

The next week was very busy, and James complained that he could hardly wait for the holidays. On Friday night, they had to work until six so James and Amy went around the corner to the café once again for dinner.

James said: "I would never have made it home; I'm too hungry. You must need something yourself, Amy."

Over their usual steak and kidney pie and salad, James told her that he had heard from his sister and that she had indeed been impressed with Amy. He had a friend from school days coming into town for the weekend, so they were going to his club for dinner.

"I'm going to miss seeing you this weekend and during our vacation week too."

"Well, the grandchildren are coming over for tea tomorrow along with their parents. It's comical how George and Stephanie always want fish-and-chips. It's a real treat for them to go down to the shop to get them.

"I've also received an invitation from Jim and Vivian Langford to visit them for a few days in Ferndene at the end of my vacation."

"And I," he laughed, "am invited to the Beaton's house that weekend and am told that the Langfords and their guest, Amy Somerset, are invited for dinner on Saturday night. So we won't be separated on that weekend after all."

They looked at each other and broke out into laughter.

Amy, wiping her eyes said: "Oh dear, such a conspiracy seems to be going on, James."

"Isn't it fun?" he laughed, patting her hand.

Barbara, Jeffery and the children arrived at Amy's flat at three on Saturday. She had straightened things up, got some laundry done, and bought some teacakes and flowers.

The children came bounding up the stairs, but knocked politely on Amy's door. As she opened it, they squealed: "Grandmother, this is smashing, coming to your place for tea. It's one of our favourite things." They each gave her a hug and a kiss. Barbara and Jeffery came in behind them, greeting her with equal affection. As they sat down, Barbara remarked on her mother's lovely flowers, which were late pink roses. After a few minutes, the children offered to go and pick up the fish-and-chips.

"Mother, you're looking a bit tired," commented Barbara. "Are you working too hard?"

"Well, it has been a very busy week, but I plan to take it easy tomorrow and just go to church and then sit and read. My vacation begins next Friday. I was wondering if you would like to go out one day during the following week to do some shopping?"

"That sounds wonderful, Mother," answered Barbara.

"I've arranged to have my hair done and to go out to lunch with Georgina on the Monday. And the Langfords have invited me for the end of the week." (Somehow she missed telling Barbara that James would be in Ferndene with the Beatons.)

Just then the children returned with the fish-and-chips.

"Look, Grandmother, we remembered to get lemon too," said Stephanie proudly.

Barbara and Amy had made the tea and put the teacakes on a plate. Everyone sat with a plate on their laps and ate their fish-and-chips. Soon the cakes too were gone, and the children had drunk their soft drinks.

"Grandmother, I would rather have this for tea than anything else I can think of—thanks," said George.

They decided to take a little walk after tea and to enjoy the cool, fresh air before heading home in the car.

It will be nice to have a quiet day tomorrow, Amy thought as she went off to sleep.

She hadn't been asleep more than two hours when she heard Mrs. Fillmore banging on her door, calling out: "Mrs. Somerset! Oh, Mrs. Somerset! Please, I need help."

Quickly Amy turned on the light and slipped on her bathrobe and slippers, and went to the door. Mrs. Fillmore was hysterical, dragging on Amy's arm. "You've got to help me. Come downstairs. My husband got up to go to the washroom and caught his foot on the mat. He hit his head on the doorway and it's bleeding and I also think he's broken his leg."

Tears were running down her face as they quickly went downstairs into her apartment.

"Oh dear, oh dear, what should I be doing?" Mrs. Fillmore moaned.

Amy took one quick look at Mr. Fillmore and knew that he needed immediate medical attention.

"I think we should dial emergency and have an ambulance sent, my dear."

Amy dialed the number and the operator assured her that help would be there shortly. She told her not to move the patient, but to staunch the bleeding with a cold, damp cloth and to put a light blanket over him. Amy went back to Mrs. Fillmore and told her to get dressed quickly, so she would be ready to go to the hospital, and meanwhile she would watch her husband.

In no time, the ambulance crew was at the door with their kit and a stretcher just as Mrs. Fillmore came out of the bedroom. They calmed down patient and wife as they examined him. They asked if he had gone unconscious.

"Oh not really, but he seemed a bit woozy," Mrs. Fillmore answered.

"Well, he certainly has broken his leg and will need some stitches on that cut. We must transport him to the hospital."

They told her which one they were taking him to. Mrs. Fillmore, with a sob in her voice, asked if Amy would go with her.

"Yes, of course, my dear," she replied. "I'll call a taxi now and run upstairs and put on some clothes." The two women arrived at the hospital about ten minutes after the ambulance, and the kindly nurse came out and said that the doctor would need about half an hour to determine what needed to be done. The nurse reassured them that she would come and get Mrs. Fillmore when her husband was settled. Mrs. Fillmore started crying again, so Amy asked where she could get her a cup of tea.

"Just down the hall on your right," answered the nurse.

"Now wait here," said Amy. "I'll be right back."

"You're so kind to help me out, Mrs. Somerset. I don't know how I would have managed without you."

They sat there until the doctor came out—a very young man, but with a kind and competent look about him.

"We'll certainly have to set that leg, but it's a clean break. We've already sewn up his cut forehead—ten stitches. I'd like to keep him here for observation over night. His blood pressure is up a bit. He says he's on medication. Can you tell me what it is and what dosage?"

"Oh yes, I've written it down, doctor," answered Mrs. Fillmore. "Luckily, I carry a note in my purse."

"I'll let you in to see him before we set that leg. He'll have to be lightly sedated, otherwise it'll be too painful for him. Just for a few minutes, and then you can return about seven in the morning. Get a bit of rest yourself."

"Thank you, doctor," she said.

She went in to see her husband to satisfy herself that he was comfortable. She cried once more on the way home in the taxi, saying: "He just looks awful but he's a proud man and didn't let on how he was suffering."

Amy offered to come back to the hospital in the morning with her, but Mrs. Fillmore wouldn't hear of it.

"Many thanks for what you've done, my dear. I think I can manage tomorrow with my son's help. The doctor says that my husband can leave by three o'clock. He's going to have to get around on crutches for a while. Good night, and thanks again."

Amy wearily climbed into bed. By then it was two-thirty in the morning. She was asleep in minutes. When she awoke the sun was shining brightly and she couldn't believe the clock showed ten-thirty.

"I guess God will forgive me for missing services this morning. It's too late now."

She spent a lazy day around her flat and, at four o'clock knocked on the Fillmore's door to see if they had returned. Their son had just brought them home and Mrs. Fillmore was preparing their tea.

"He seems fine my dear Mrs. Somerset. I thank you again."

Amy replied: "I'll stop in during the week to see how he's doing. Goodbye for now."

She went to the grocer's and picked up a nice meat pie and a salad for her dinner. She was in bed by nine o'clock and slept the night through.

James told her the next morning that he had an enjoyable visit with his friend, and was surprised to hear of all Amy's activities.

"So much for a quiet weekend," he said.

They were both looking forward to their vacations, but James told her that he would miss her terribly. However, for the present they had to face a very busy week and they were exhausted and ready for their holiday by Friday night.

20

Amy was glad just to have time to think and to relax. She did mundane things for the whole weekend, the grandchildren being occupied with sport and a birthday party.

Mr. Fillmore was hobbling around on his crutches and his face still had an ugly bruise from his fall. Amy brought them a lovely meat pie, some tartlets and a newspaper for him. With tears in her eyes, Mrs. Fillmore gave her a hug and a kiss and said: "You are such a sweetheart."

On Monday, Amy and Georgina had appointments with Giorgio for a full treatment—haircuts and manicures. "What a nice way for me to begin my week," he said to them. "Let me get you some tea or coffee."

They both chose tea and felt themselves in the lap of luxury. They had lunch at a very smart restaurant and even had a daring glass of wine. This made them giggly, and it further relaxed them. Next, they had an appointment with Madame Zolie at two o'clock, and they both were in a buying mood.

"I haven't been here in a few months. With fall coming, I

would like to have something new for the office and for going out," stated Amy firmly.

Madame Zolie was ready for them and, being a true saleswoman, had picked out a few things in advance for them to try on. For Georgina, she had chosen a lovely moss green dress and jacket with velvet piping. With Georgina's green eyes, the dress was very becoming. She was very satisfied and decided just to browse around while Amy was served. Amy chose a dress in soft blue with ruching around a "V" neckline. The belt was a perfect match in soft kid.

"Oh, Madame Zolie, you always pick out the best things," said Amy appreciatively.

Madame also had chosen a wool suit in bright navy with a muted grey and blue pin-striped blouse. "Very appropriate for the office or an informal dinner, Mrs. Somerset." It was irresistible to Amy but she decided to put it on lay-away so as not to strain her budget.

Madame Zolie smiled with satisfaction as she said: "Now how about some tea and a biscuit before you go home. My clerk will wrap up your purchases for you."

Amy and Georgina had enjoyed a marvellous day and felt like pampered royals. They both took taxis home, giving each other a hug before they separated.

Amy hung up her purchase and admired it as she had tea and toast that evening. Tomorrow would be a day of rest.

The day dawned sunny and warm. She did a leisurely grocery shopping, taking time to talk to the grocer and his daughter. On her return, she stowed her purchases and sat in her favourite chair, put her feet up and read the morning paper.

As she sipped her tea, she could not help but reflect on her relationship with James and the direction it was taking. That they shared a mutual love was no longer in doubt, but she badly needed approval and support, mainly from Barbara. She vowed to bare her feelings when she and Barbara met for lunch the next day.

They met at the restaurant at twelve-thirty, and Barbara's first question was: "Are you enjoying your holiday week, Mother?"

"Oh yes. I'm having a grand time. Georgina and I went to the hairdresser's on Monday, had lunch and then went to Madame Zolie's. We each bought a lovely outfit."

She then told Barbara about how well Mr. Fillmore was getting along. They each had a glass of wine and Amy said: "I'm glad I don't go out for too many lunches. I find that I get tipsy very easily as I get older."

Amy wanted to consult Barbara about her relationship with James, but could not find an opening to explore her feelings. Instead, they talked mostly about Jeffery and the children. They went to the shoe department at Harrod's after lunch. Amy found a wonderful pair of Italian-made pumps, very comfortable and good soft leather.

"I have to buy good shoes. The cheaper ones don't last and are uncomfortable to wear all day long," she said. They both bought some make-up, helping each other with colour under the scrutiny of the haughty salesgirl. They did a bit more shopping and had tea and cakes in the café, but never got around to the serious conversation that Amy wanted so badly.

Amy packed for the weekend trip three times, but kept changing her mind. James called to say that he would pick her up on Saturday morning at about ten and also that he would drive her home on Sunday.

It was raining in the morning so James carefully held an

umbrella over her as he carried her luggage out to the car. As they drove off, he said: "Now Amy, did you miss me as much as I missed you? It has been a whole week you know."

Amy, rather flustered, replied: "Well, we certainly do spend so much time together. I guess I did miss you a little, James."

"Let's hear some enthusiasm, please," he joked, "or my feelings will be hurt."

She couldn't help but laugh.

"Now tell me what you did during the past week," he asked. She gave him a good accounting of her week, emphasizing that she took ample time for rest.

He told her that a weekend with Genevieve was more than enough. He didn't tell her that she had given him the third degree about the seriousness of his relationship with Amy.

"I had a good game of golf with Ian and enjoyed my time at my friend's. We only played two games of golf because it rained one day. We had many long conversations and reminisced about 'the good old days' but I was glad to get back to London for a couple of days of genuine rest."

The rain started to come down in earnest and James had to concentrate on his driving.

"Are you looking forward to this weekend?" he asked, when the rain finally abated.

Amy answered: "As you know, Jim and Vivian are old friends. He helped take care of my William before he died. Vivian and I were friends in the same bridge club and in the Women's Institute. She loves flowers like I do, and has a lovely garden."

"The Beatons are having us all together for dinner tonight. Doesn't it bother you to go back to your house?" he asked.

"Oh no, I still love Bower House of course, but thanks to you, I'm getting a wonderful rent, and between Tilly and the Beatons my house is in good hands. In fact, I am looking forward to tonight."

"To seeing me again, or your house?" he asked with a smile.

"Now stop teasing," she answered with a smile too.

Doctor Jim was out on an emergency case, but Vivian welcomed them both. The rain had stopped. The sun had come out and everything looked newly washed. The drops of rain sparkled like diamonds on the leaves.

James carried Amy's suitcase into the house, and Vivian asked him if he could stay for a visit.

"No, no," he said, "the Beatons are expecting me soon. Thank you."

"Well, we'll see you tonight," said Vivian, "and I've asked everyone to an early tea tomorrow, so you can be on your way back to London. I feel that the Beatons have done all the entertaining, and that we should do something."

"Goodbye for now," waved James, smiling at both. Vivian hugged Amy and told her she hoped that Jim would be back around lunchtime.

Amy went up to the lovely guest room overlooking the garden, and hung up the new dress that she had bought this week at Madame Zolie's. What woman can resist wearing a new dress as soon as possible? she asked herself. She put away her other things in the bureau, combed her hair in place and went downstairs.

Vivian was in the kitchen, stirring a wonderful-smelling soup.

"Oh, I can hardly wait for lunch," said Amy. "Just the aroma from that soup makes me hungry."

"I thought it would be nice for Jim to have something good and hot when he gets home, too," added Vivian. She showed

Amy around the back garden for a few minutes, pointing out the autumnal flowers. There were still a few pink dahlias left and some late roses and rose hips.

They went back in for lunch and ate their soup. Amy tried to recount some of the more notable things, like spilling tea on James, the incident with her landlord, and shopping with Georgina and Barbara. She avoided talking about the office.

Vivian noticed that James's name cropped up often, and that the two of them seemed to be spending a good deal of time together outside the office. Just then, Jim came in. He had finished the emergency case, and the patient was going to be fine. He wouldn't mind some of that delicious-smelling soup right now.

He gave Amy a kiss on the cheek and remarked on how healthy and rested she looked.

"How can you be breathing in those foul fumes all day in London and look like that?" he asked. She laughed, saying that she had been given the week off and had enjoyed a good rest.

Vivian also served a chicken salad with fresh hot rolls, followed by two cheeses and biscuits.

"We're not expected at the Beatons until six-thirty, so dinner will be later tonight," Vivian announced.

Jim had dried off the patio furniture and said to Amy: "It has warmed up considerably since this morning and I'm prescribing some fresh air."

They had an interesting chat together, Vivian describing some of the things that Amy was missing in the village life.

"Mrs. Epsom-Smythe is proud as a peacock now," she laughed. "She won second prize for the flower arranging."

"Now tell Amy who won first prize," said Doctor Jim. "My darling talented wife. I am very proud of her. You know she loves flowers."

"Congratulations, dear," said Amy, giving her a hug.

Soon it was four o'clock and time for an early tea, but only tea and biscuits, so as to preserve their appetites. As Amy dressed for dinner, she admired again her new dress and wondered if James would notice. They arrived at the Beatons at six-thirty. Sir John greeted them at the door.

"Welcome to your home, Amy," he laughed. "Does that still sound strange to you? Hello Vivian and Jim."

Lady Jane and James were in the living room. She greeted her new guests warmly.

"Isn't this wonderful to be able to get together again?" Lady Jane said.

James, with a very warm smile for Amy remarked: "This must be especially nice for you to come here tonight. You are looking extra chic. Is that a new dress?" He greeted the others, smiling and shaking their hands. "So we meet again. The day has turned out to be so beautiful."

Amy looked around the living room, which had a rosy glow in the setting sun. It certainly was a beautiful room and she realized again how much she missed it.

Sir John motioned: "Please sit down while I get some drinks."

"May I help you?" asked James.

The orders were taken.

"No sherry for you, Amy, I presume?" James said with a knowing smile.

"Just a light gin and tonic, please. You know how I take it." She smiled back at James.

Soon Tilly came in with some cheese straws, which she passed around.

"I am so glad to see you, Tilly," greeted Amy. "I'll come into the kitchen later and talk with you."

After about fifteen or twenty minutes, they all walked towards the dining room, James taking Amy's arm. Lady Beaton sat them side by side across from Vivian and Jim and she and Sir John sat on the ends. A shrimp cocktail was served first with a marvellous sauce.

"It's so nice to be here tonight with all of you," Amy said. "I still consider Ferndene my home, and returning to it and my old friends is always a joy. However, I must admit that, after a week off, I'm also looking forward to returning to work on Monday."

There was much laughter at some of the stories told during dinner. Sir John was truly a gracious host. 'He must have been a wonderful diplomat,' thought Amy.

Tilly's niece was serving once again and the next course consisted of sliced beef tenderloin with a savoury sauce, and broccoli as a vegetable. James looked at Amy and noticed that she was bravely trying to eat a little of her broccoli. He pointed at some imaginary bird outside the window and deftly transferred the rest onto his plate. Only Amy saw his manoeuvre and she had to put her napkin over her mouth to prevent herself from laughing out loud. To get control, she drank a sip of wine and listened intently to a story that Jim was telling.

A delicious pudding was served, and they all returned to the living room for coffee and tea. James, always a teller of stories too, entertained everyone for the whole while. Soon, it was time to go and Amy asked if she might take a few minutes to talk to Tilly.

Tilly was busy cleaning up, but was delighted to greet Amy and she gave her a hug and a kiss on the cheek. "You certainly look beautiful in that dress. You seem to look younger and happier every time I see you."

"I truly am happy, Tilly. With my job and the busy weekends

too, I don't have time to be anything else. It is nice to see Barbara, Jeffery and the grandchildren often and Georgina and Basil too. I go out to dinner and to concerts on the weekends, and have just enjoyed a week's holiday."

"Well, I like your boss Mr. Carstairs very much. I do miss seeing the grandchildren. They must be really growing," Tilly added.

"Oh yes," said Amy, "George is as tall as I am."

Amy promised to write her again, they had one final hug, and Amy returned to the others.

Everyone was saying good night, and as Amy said her thank yous to the Beatons, James pressed her hand and said quietly: "It's so nice to see you Amy. I'll see you again at the Langfords for tea tomorrow. Good night until then."

His attention had not gone unnoticed by anyone. Sir John said to his wife with a knowing smile: "I think they're going to make a match."

"I'm sure of it," she agreed.

Vivian and Jim also discussed it later and came to the same conclusion.

"I will be so happy for Amy. I hope she's ready to receive his proposal when it comes," Vivian mused.

As Amy went to sleep, she laughed to herself at the sly way that James had taken her unwanted broccoli.

21

Amy and her hosts attended church together the next morning. As they came out, Jane Barnaby came up to them saying: “Hello, Amy. Did Doctor Jim here tell you that my ‘baby’ turned out to be twins again? Both girls!”

“No, I didn’t,” said Jim. “I thought you might want to do that yourself.”

“Well, they were born in August on a stormy night and Doctor Jim was wonderful. They were a couple of weeks early, but they’re very healthy now. My husband is at home with the children right now, so I must hurry back. I’m so pleased to see you Amy, and to share our good news.”

“Congratulations, Jane dear. You must be very proud.”

As Jane left, Doctor Jim remarked on what a wonderful family they were. A moment later, James and the Beatons came up to them. James said: “What a lovely day. We are looking forward to tea this afternoon.”

“Yes indeed,” agreed the Beatons. “We’ll be there at two-thirty.”

Mrs. Epsom-Smythe joined the group. "Well hello everyone. Isn't it a fine day? So nice to see you visiting, Amy. You are looking well." Her curiosity was satisfied as she was introduced to James.

"Well, I must go now, I see my husband waiting over there. Goodbye," she called as she sailed out of sight.

Amy went home with Vivian and Jim. After a light lunch of vichyssoise, cheese and biscuits, she said that she must go upstairs to pack and get ready to return to London.

The guests did indeed arrive at two-thirty, glad to see one another again. James had a special soft smile for Amy that made her blush, but she smiled in return.

Vivian had baked delicious scones to accompany their tea, but both James and Amy passed on the sherry. James said: "It makes me too sleepy. I must be alert for the drive home."

They sat on the patio, as the afternoon was unusually warm for late September. They ate until all were sated, then James stood and announced that they must go before the traffic got too heavy. Amy and James both said their goodbyes and thank yous, and started off on their way home.

"Did you enjoy the dinner last night?" asked James.

She started to reply: "Oh yes—" but she caught the gleam in his eyes and started to laugh. "James, you are the limit—taking the broccoli off my plate when you thought that no one was looking." They both laughed uproariously.

He took her hand and said: "Now I couldn't have you disgrace me by leaving the broccoli, or worse yet, hiding it under something." After a brief silence, he added: "How lovely you looked in that dress last night."

"Oh, thank you. Georgina and I had a grand time on Monday, getting our hair done, going out for a tipsy lunch, and then shopping at Madame Zolie's. We do love shopping there."

"Well, I can see why. I really missed you this week, Amy," said James, again glancing at her face, which had coloured up.

She didn't know what to say, but managed: "It will be hard to get down to business tomorrow. But the fact is that I missed you, too. You've become much more to me than just a boss."

After this frank admission, they drove along in silence for several miles. Finally, James spoke up: "Next Saturday, there is a hot air balloon ascension about an hour and a half drive north of the city. It starts at eleven in the morning. Would you like to come with me?" he asked.

"Now James, where do you get all these interesting invitations that are impossible for me to turn down? I have never seen a balloon up close and it would be amazing to see a whole group of them. Please let me pack us a lovely lunch in a hamper. You are always entertaining me."

He drove to her flat and carried her suitcase upstairs. With a grin, he said: "See that you're on time for work tomorrow, Mrs. Somerset."

The next few days flew by. There was so much work to catch up on since they had been away on vacation.

Soon, it was Saturday and the day was clear and bright, perfect weather for the balloon ascension. The sky was blue and cloudless. The leaves were starting to turn colour and the air was crisp. Amy had a fine lunch ready, prepared from gourmet items that she had bought the day before from the grocer's.

James was at her flat at nine-thirty and came upstairs to carry down the hamper.

"What is in this hamper? Am I expected to eat everything in here?" he joked. "It is very heavy."

"You probably will," she answered with a chuckle.

As they drove out of London, James remarked on how comfortable it was to have light traffic. He was dressed casually in a sweater and slacks.

"You look quite handsome in that outfit, James. I only see you in suits or formal wear usually."

"You look more than handsome, my dear Amy. I've never seen you wear slacks before."

They both smiled over the exchange of compliments. As they arrived at the balloon site, there was every colour of the rainbow scattered about a large field. James parked the car and they walked around the roped-in area.

"Let's watch that fellow inflate his balloon, Amy," he said, taking her hand.

They walked close to a large basket tethered to the ground, where three men were carefully inflating their brilliantly-striped balloon. A group of young boys was watching, and being held back by their parents. Some of the balloons were already starting to ascend.

"What a magnificent sight! 'Awesome' is the only word to adequately describe it," exclaimed Amy.

The balloons were going up higher and drifting off in the sky on a light easterly breeze. James spied a sign that read: "Balloon Rides—Come Sail With Me."

"Would you be brave enough to try a balloon ride with me? I've wanted to do it since I was a little boy. Please say yes, I crave adventure," he pleaded.

"Well, I don't know," she answered with considerable doubt in her voice.

James took her by the elbow as he whispered in her ear: "Now, that fellow looks completely trustworthy, don't you think?"

With much persuasion, she finally weakened. They climbed

aboard with two other people and the balloonist and his helper, and soon the ropes were loosed and they started to rise. The ground was left behind and they all experienced the elation of a bird's-eye view of checkered fields and shrinking houses.

James kept hold of her shaking hand. Eventually, she relaxed, and said with genuine feeling: "What a spectacular view. I'm so glad I came for the ride."

Soon the balloon drifted slowly down toward earth to the appointed spot on the ground where helpers caught the dragging lines. Amy's legs were a bit wobbly as she got off, so James tenderly took her arm and escorted her to the waiting car.

"May I tell you again, my dear Amy, how I admire you. No other person I know is as brave as you. Thank you for sharing this adventure with me. Now admit it, you did enjoy the ride a little bit, didn't you?"

Amy laughed out loud. "You did have to press me some but I'm very grateful that you did, and will remember it forever."

At that, he kissed her hand and laughed along with her.

They both were ready for lunch, so James carried the basket to a shady spot under a tree. Amy spread out the brightly coloured cloth and set out the food in a most appealing display. James ate everything that she had brought, declaring his pleasure after each course.

This is the perfect time, James thought to himself. He looked at Amy with a special glow in his eyes.

"Amy, I enjoy your company so much. Have you had the suspicion that I've fallen in love with you? Because I have, deeply."

At that he took both her hands and asked: "Do you love me too, Amy? Please say that you do."

"Oh yes, James. I've tried to resist my feelings. However, now I can say that I've fallen very much in love with you too. I always look forward to our times together. Thank you for your patience and your persistence."

At that, he brought out a box from his pocket, opened it and displayed a beautiful solitaire diamond ring.

"Will you marry me, Amy dear?" he said with a husky voice.

"Oh yes, James dear, without reservation."

Kissing her hand, he put the ring on her finger. As they went to kiss, Amy put her hand in the pâté. They both looked down and laughed. He cleaned off her hand, saying: "Please don't ever change, my darling Amy. I love you just the way you are." They gave each other a long and loving kiss.

They sat on the picnic blanket holding hands, talking, losing track of time, and discussing future plans. James wanted to tell everyone immediately and to get married at Christmas. Amy agreed that they should share the joyous news with family and friends at once, and that Christmas season would be a perfect time for the wedding.

"I have loved you almost from the first day that you began work in my office. But my admiration and respect grew as I observed your efficiency, cheerfulness and the brave manner in which you set out to protect your beautiful home.

"But, no more skimping for you, my dear. I've never told you, but I inherited a handsome sum from my father who founded our firm, and my practice has also been rewarding, yet I've lived as a reclusive bachelor. These savings should enable us to maintain two homes, mine in London and your beloved Bower House, and still afford to travel to our heart's content. For openers, I would like to suggest a warm spot like Barbados for our honeymoon."

"But all of that seems so extravagant. Everyone is going to say that I married you for your money," she replied.

"But you and I know better, my dear. We are marrying only for love." And he kissed her again.

They packed up the car but were in no hurry to return to London. Instead, they stopped at a charming little inn and talked some more over a light dinner. As evening came, James suggested that they stop at Barbara and Jeffery's to share their news. When Amy seemed just a little hesitant, James asked what was troubling her.

"James, our engagement will probably be seen by our families and friends as the poorest kept secret in the land. Georgina has questioned me about our intentions, and the others have only to observe our recent conduct to guess that this was in the wind. But most of all, I feel badly that I've been unable to share my feelings with Barbara. I've tried many times to raise the subject but I just never could find the right opening."

"I shouldn't worry, Amy. Barbara and her family love you and want only the best for you. Let's call ahead to tell them that we are stopping in shortly to share some wonderful news with them. By the time we arrive, I think that our announcement will not come as a complete surprise."

"We knew that love was blossoming between you two," cried Barbara upon being told the news. First, she kissed her mother and then James. "You are so suited to each other and I'm positive that you'll be very happy."

"As long as we have your blessing, Barbara," said James. "I do love your mother, and will take very good care of her."

Jeffery was pounding James on the back and shaking his hand, saying: "Well, well. We knew there would be a wedding soon, didn't we Barbara? You two were heading for it. It wasn't hard to tell."

Amy responded: "I guess that I've been wrong to not share my feelings with you and seek your counsel. I see now that your approval and blessing were always available if only I'd opened up to you both."

"This is going to be a very merry Christmas, Grandmother," chirped Stephanie. "What should we call you? Sir?" she asked James.

"Well, let's start out with 'James' for now. I feel too young to be called Grandfather," and they all laughed.

They called Georgina and Basil from Amy's flat and were given many congratulations again. Amy and James sat on the sofa, talking some more and figuring who else should be called and how to break the news at the office. At about nine-thirty, James said that he should leave. Other matters would just have to wait.

"See you tomorrow, my darling," he said, and they kissed once more.

Amy shed a few tears as she got into bed that night, but felt that William would be happy for her. Two years seemed like an indecently short time to remain a widow, but in other ways it seemed like an eternity. The important thing was that she really loved James; such a kind, funny man. He would be a wonderful husband.

22

The next morning they were both at the office early. James shut his office door, pulled Amy into his arms and kissed her and said: "Are you as happy as I am, my darling?"

"Oh yes James. I feel totally sure about this. I love you very much. My family seems so happy for us too."

"Well, we have many more people to tell—my sister for one—my friends, the other partners."

"And I must tell Vivian and Jim, Tilly and my landlady. And, one of us must tell the Beatons."

Giving her one more kiss, he said: "Well, for now we must get down to business, but I intend to take up more of your evenings, Mrs. Somerset."

"I wanted to ask how your friend is doing—the one that keeps giving us tickets to the theatre?"

"Well if you must know, he was an invention of mine—an excuse to get you to come out with me more often," he confessed.

"Oh James, you are such a rascal. Any other confessions to make?"

"That's it," he said, kissing her again. "Now let's get to work; maybe tonight we can go to our favourite café around the corner and make more plans."

They worked very hard that day but stopped at five. As they were eating their dinner, James announced: "I called my sister today to tell her the news. She's very happy for us and said it was about time I got married. She likes you very much, and will feel privileged to have you as a sister-in-law, especially after I told her your background at dinner that night."

"James, you didn't have to do that, you know. I like people to take me as I am."

"You don't know my sister. She's truly a snob, and it did her a world of good." He laughed heartily. "She wants us to come down to visit for a weekend as soon as possible. We'll both have to consult our busy social calendars, although most of our engagements seem to be mutual of late."

"I hope that she and I get on well together, since we both love the same man."

"You and I are a team now," he smiled as he took her hand. "I won't let anyone hurt your feelings."

"Thank you, James. You're a great comfort to me."

They decided to be married on the Saturday between Christmas and New Year's. James said he knew the manager at Claridge's and would reserve for a luncheon.

"Would you like to arrange the ceremony at the church near your flat or is there another that you would prefer?"

"The church near me is a very lovely old building and holds about two hundred people, but we shouldn't feel that we have to fill it. Please, let's have a smaller wedding."

They totalled up a preliminary guest list, which came to eighty people—a size that suited them both.

"And how does a month in Barbados sound for our honeymoon? I'm told that it's a lovely island with an ideal winter climate, and very English."

"Oh yes," she answered with shining eyes. "I've never been there. That would be wonderful."

"We must go to the travel agency together and see what flights can be arranged and enquire about accommodations. I would like to ask my brother-in-law to be my best man. My sister would certainly be angry if I didn't. In any case, I consider Ian a good friend."

"And I'll ask Barbara to be my matron of honour, and Stephanie to be the flower girl."

"Perhaps we should ask George to be the ring bearer, or he will feel left out," offered James, "and Jeffery to be an usher."

"That would very thoughtful to include Jeffery. As for George, he may feel that he is too old," Amy worried.

"Let him decide for himself," said James diplomatically. "I must also make a formal announcement to the staff, although I'm sure that all of them already know."

Amy said: "There are so many things to think of. My head is in a whirl."

"Between the two of us, we shall manage just fine." He grasped her hand tightly. "I think that my efficient secretary will begin making her lists, and between Barbara and Georgina, you'll have plenty of help."

"Yes, they can be depended upon without question."

Sure enough, Barbara dropped by the next day at noon with a bridal book, listing all the things to do and a checklist to guide a couple through their wedding preparations.

"Now, I want you two ladies to go out to lunch," ordered

James. "I can spare my secretary until one-thirty. I have a luncheon meeting with a client."

"I called the Vicar, James, and he said the church is free that day, and the ceremony can be at noon. Since we are of the same faith and a mature couple, as he kindly put it, there will be no problem. He wants to see us on Thursday night to discuss details with us."

"That's fine, Amy. Now you two get along. I'm sure you have much planning to do."

The ladies wasted no time in finding a quiet booth at a restaurant nearby where they could talk freely.

"I'm so happy for you, Mother," said Barbara giving her a hug.

"It doesn't upset you that I want to re-marry, dear?" There was a tremor in her voice.

"Mother, my father was a wonderful man and we shall never forget him of course, but you must think of yourself and start a new life with James. He is just the right one for you and will take good care of you. Now no more of this talk Mother. Let's do some planning. Gracious, you're getting married in two months and there's much to do."

"Will you be my matron-of-honour, Barbara?" asked Amy.

"I would be honoured and happy to, Mother. Let's start by calling Georgina and Madame Zolie and plan to make a day of it on Saturday picking out your wedding outfit. You can also shop for your trousseau clothes and I'd like to choose my dress. We can also have a first talk with the florist when our dress colours are set."

"Oh dear, there's so much to think of," worried Amy again.

"We have the wedding planner book," Barbara reminded her. "You said that James was going to book the luncheon, so we'll have him set aside some rooms for out-of-town guests too."

They nibbled away at their salads, both being too excited to eat very much. They stopped at the printer's and picked up some sample invitations. Amy went back to the office and she and James finished up a good day's work at five-thirty.

"How about taking an hour or so for dinner with me at another café I know. You can tell me how you and Barbara got along and we can discuss more plans."

"That would be lovely," she answered. "There certainly seems to be much to talk about."

"It would be fun to elope," James interjected with a smile. "But we must think of everyone's feelings I suppose."

James reported that he had inquired at the hotel about having cocktails and a luncheon commencing at one-thirty. The food manager would be sending over some sample menus to aid in their choices.

Amy told him that she was going to Madame Zolie's on Saturday with Barbara and Georgina to pick out a wedding outfit and a few things for her trousseau.

"Now Amy, remember I don't want you to hold back. Make me proud of my beautiful bride. Buy some lovely things for our trip. I know that money can't replace good taste, but I've heard that it makes decisions easier."

"Oh James, I'm not used to spending much money on clothes. I will feel so guilty."

"Please, Amy, let me enjoy seeing you in all your new finery," he said with a smile and a squeeze to her hand.

They talked about invitations, and easily agreed on the form. Amy undertook to meet with the printer to draft wording. James heartily approved of her picking out the flowers with Barbara and Georgina, since they were such experts.

"I would love to have you see my—I mean our house again. I

want to invite Barbara, Jeffery and the children over on Sunday for tea. And you too of course," James added jokingly.

"That's very thoughtful, James."

He kissed her hand.

"I really must go home soon. I must make my calls and share our good news," she said.

"I don't really think that any of them will be surprised," he said with a smile.

Of course, everyone told Amy that they had been expecting the announcement for some time. She told them the date of the ceremony and that the invitations would be out in about two weeks. Everyone was very excited and happy for them. Tilly had a good cry of course. The Beatons offered their sincere congratulations to Amy. They said that they would call James to congratulate him too.

That evening, Mrs. Fillmore cried when Amy told her the news. She had seen the handsome gentleman out her window, driving up in his grand car to pick Amy up or drop her off.

"Would you come to the wedding?" asked Amy, hugging her.

"Oh my, I know it will be a grand affair. What would I wear?"

"I'm sure you'll find something nice. Why don't you treat yourself to a new hat? Hats are still very popular at weddings. With your lovely hair showing, everyone will think the Queen Mum has come."

She laughed heartily and added: "I'll just remind my husband that it's been ten years since I've had a new outfit."

Amy laughed along with her and said good night.

It had been a hectic few days and she was totally spent. She took a long hot bath and went to bed very early.

They went to see the Vicar, who welcomed the opportunity to unite a mature couple. He was a jolly elderly man with a fringe of white hair, like a halo that had slipped.

"It's wonderful to have found each other later in life and know that you'll spend your twilight years together." He gave them a choice of ceremonies, readings and hymns, and said he wanted to see them again in three weeks. There would also be a wedding rehearsal the night before the ceremony.

Some of Amy's fellow secretaries asked her to take a few minutes one lunch hour so they could see her ring and congratulate her. They also wanted her to pick a date for a shower. Josie gave her an extra hug and said how very happy she was for Amy and Mr. Carstairs.

On Friday night, James took her out for dinner again and suggested that they set up a schedule with their dates on it. "We have so many things to remember. This old bachelor is as happy as can be, but this wedding business is getting to be overwhelming."

"Maybe we should elope, James dear," she said, mimicking his prior suggestion.

"No, we're committed now, my darling Amy, and we must somehow support each other through this. Are you and the girls going shopping tomorrow?"

"Yes, Barbara is picking us up. We have an appointment with Madame Zolie at ten in the morning."

"Now, don't tire yourself out too much tomorrow. I've set up the tea party for Sunday with Barbara, Jeffery and the children. I must be on best terms with them. I don't want them to have any doubts about me."

They talked about their progress to date on the details of the wedding, and this seemed to ease their minds.

"Let's make next Wednesday night our time for addressing

the invitations. If my houseman serves an early dinner, we can do them at my place." Amy agreed.

Saturday morning arrived, after a rather restless night for Amy. The girls were equally excited. Madame Zolie greeted them and congratulated Amy with a kiss and hug.

"It will be a pleasure to choose a beautiful dress for a beautiful bride. We should have a wonderful couple of hours. First and most important of course is your choice for the wedding dress."

She brought out a pale beige silk suit, with grosgrain trim on the collar and sleeves, which Amy tried on. On her hair, she placed a wispy veil held on the sides by two combs, and a flat grosgrain bow on top. The effect was stunning.

"You must have matching shoes of course," added Madame Zolie.

Barbara and Georgina expressed their full approval of the ensemble. "Nothing could be more beautiful!" they agreed.

For Barbara, she had chosen a similar suit in a medium rose shade, with no hat. "Just a lovely bouquet of mixed pink roses for you to carry, Madame; and for the bride, a bouquet of cream roses."

"Oh Madame Zolie, your taste is impeccable. You've made it so easy for me." Through tears, Amy thanked and hugged her.

For her friend, Georgina, Madame had selected a maroon silk shantung suit with diamante buttons, which, with her dark colouring, looked wonderful.

"Now, we must choose some items for your trousseau. Monsieur Carstairs called to inform me that you are travelling to Barbados for a month and that I must not allow you to skimp in any way. Versatile outfits would be best, with soft fabrics for easy packing. I have chosen a blue summer suit with a matching shell and a lightweight blue raincoat. Here is a lovely scarf to use with it, and also a light print blouse as an alternative. I know your other clothes will fit in with these. It will make a lovely travelling outfit for going away."

For evening wear, Madame Zolie had chosen a grey pleated outfit that could be laid flat with tissue in her suitcase and come out wrinkle-free—also white slacks and top. A soft gauzy print dress in navy with ruffled neck and hemline also looked very chic.

"Stop, stop!" Amy exclaimed. "This is more than enough. Madame Zolie, I am sure that James didn't mean for me to spend all of his money."

"Monsieur told me to make you be generous to yourself. I took it as an order."

Amy laughed. "Now what can you do with such an outrageous man?"

At that, Madame held up a stunning pale blue peignoir set with silk ribbons threaded around the collar. Amy was so overwhelmed that she sat down and cried. Barbara and Georgina both hugged her and called her a fairy tale princess and encouraged her to buy the complete trousseau spread before her.

"Mother, I think you're a little overwhelmed. We need a break and a good lunch. Let's stop for now. Madame Zolie, you have done a magnificent job. We'll convince her to take everything. Please have them sent to my house on Monday. She'll have settled down by then."

Barbara and Georgina took Amy to a fine old restaurant and had the hostess seat them in a back corner. They made Amy order a light gin and tonic and a substantial lunch.

"Now relax, Mother," Barbara said as she put her arm around her mother. "I know you're going through a busy and emotional time but you must allow yourself to enjoy it."

Georgina added: "We're here for you as support and together we'll get you through the next two months. Everyone is so happy for you and we all love James too. He is a truly wonderful man."

Amy finally calmed down and managed to eat a decent lunch and to enjoy her drink.

"James and I want to ask Jeffery to usher and we also want Stephanie to be the flower girl at the wedding, and George to be the ring bearer if he doesn't think that he is too old."

"Well, I know Stephanie will be thrilled Mother, but George must make up his own mind. He surely won't want to be left out. Jeffery would be honoured to be an usher, I'm sure."

"That's exactly what James said. We will ask them all tomorrow."

Georgina commented again on the beautiful bridal outfit that Madame Zolie had chosen for Amy.

"Oh yes," said Amy enthusiastically. "It's just perfect. And your outfits suit both of you wonderfully too." With a smile, she added: "The guests may have difficulty identifying the bride."

When they felt fully recovered, they went to Amy's favourite florist shop. Since all three were very knowledgeable about flowers, it took no time at all to choose the flowers.

By the time Barbara dropped her off at her flat, Amy felt completely drained of energy. James called just after five to see how they had fared. She scolded him for being so extravagant. "Imagine calling Madame Zolie and giving her carte blanche like that!"

"Do you still love me, my dearest Amy?" he asked coyly.

"Of course I do, you silly old thing, but you're being a spendthrift and I'm not used to that."

She told him how easy it was to pick out the lovely flowers and that Barbara and Georgina had been of great help. She was almost too tired to eat, but managed some scrambled eggs, toast and tea, followed by a long soak in a hot tub before an early bedtime.

23

Tea was to be at James's townhouse at three o'clock on Sunday. He joined Amy for the eleven o'clock service at the church where they were to be married. She then returned with James to his home to await the arrival of Barbara, Jeffery and the children.

James greeted them with smiles, embraces and handshakes. The houseman, introduced as Fenwick, took their coats and James ushered them into the living room. The family was all agog to see the groom-to-be's house and Amy's future home.

"You have a lovely home, James," said Barbara, "so bright and spacious."

"Yes indeed, James," added Jeffery.

Stephanie and George were using their best manners and Amy surmised that they had been given strict orders in advance. She was very proud of their mature behaviour. Fenwick returned with a large tiered tray of sandwiches and biscuits, a plate of scones with two pots of jam and cream and finally a tea tray and soft drinks for the children.

Everyone exclaimed over the delicious food and George, with his mouth full blurted: "I say, this is something wonderful!"

His father gave him a glaring look, which told him that he was to be quiet while eating.

Amy and James looked at each other smiling and Amy said to Stephanie: "We were wondering, dear, if you would like to be the flower girl at our wedding?"

Stephanie turned three shades of pink and looking at her mother exclaimed: "Oh, Grandmother that would be the most exciting thing! Thank you both."

Barbara added: "Perhaps Madame Zolie could come up with a lovely outfit for you to wear, darling."

"I'm sure she can," agreed Amy. "And thank you for saying yes, Stephanie."

James asked Jeffery to be an usher and he responded enthusiastically. George was looking a little perturbed at all the attention that his sister was getting, when James said to him: "And you George. Would you mind helping to usher the guests to their seats along with your father, and if you don't think you are too old, also act as ring bearer?"

"I would be happy to usher," answered George immediately, "but what does a ring bearer do?"

"Well, he carries the rings on a pillow up to the front of the church and then stands to one side until the Vicar asks for them," James explained.

George looked at his father questioningly.

"It's up to you, son."

"That seems to be a big responsibility. I'm sure I'll make a botch of it and drop them."

Everybody laughed.

"The rings are tied to a small cushion, so it won't happen, darling," Amy assured him.

"Yes? Then I will do both, Grandmother and—er—James."

"I was wondering if we could be fitted for formal rentals a week from next Saturday," James enquired. "Jeffery, my brother-in-law, and also you, George, and I will wear tuxedoes. After the fitting, I'll take all of the men to my club for lunch."

"That sounds fine with us, George, doesn't it?" said Jeffery.

"Of course Father," said George, feeling very grown-up to be treated like a man.

"The same day, we'll have Stephanie try on her dress, Barbara, and go out to lunch with Georgina," said Amy. "Perhaps next week you could take Stephanie to Madame Zolie and give her the challenge of producing something beautiful for a young lady."

"Amy and I are going down to my sister's place for the weekend next Saturday," said James. "Genevieve and Ian would like to get to know her better."

James then took everyone on a tour of the house and they were impressed with the tasteful furnishings. They remarked on James's painting by A.A. Lebrandt, which was so similar to Amy's.

"Is yours worth more than Grandmother's, sir?" asked George innocently. Diplomatically, James answered: "Probably about the same, George," noticing that Jeffery was glaring at his son again.

"Well, we must be going, James," said Barbara. "Thank you so much for the tea and the tour."

"Yes, thank you for the lovely tea, sir," added Stephanie, putting on her grown-up manners.

"We'll look forward to seeing you a week Saturday then, James," Jeffery said shaking James's hand.

"Shall we say ten o'clock? I will pick you both up," said James.

Amy decided to ride with her family to save James the trip.

As they said goodbye, James gave Amy a kiss and added that he would see her tomorrow.

On the way home in the car, George got a good talking to about his manners. Stephanie sat there holding Grandmother's hand saying: "Thank you, Grandmother, for asking me to be the flower girl."

After the exhausting weekend, Amy was glad to enjoy a quiet evening in her flat, reading a book until sleep came.

Lady Beaton dialled the office on Monday to see if James and Amy would be free three weeks from Saturday. Their friends in Ferndene wished to have a party for them. James and Amy could stay with the Beatons at Bower House where the party was to be held. Amy checked her calendar and also asked James before graciously accepting.

A few minutes later, James asked Amy if she was free in three weeks on the Wednesday night for a dinner to be put on by the partners and their wives. She checked the calendar again and said "yes."

"I hope that you're writing this down, dear."

"Oh yes. That is the only way we can remember, James."

The secretaries were also giving Amy a shower at lunch time two weeks before the wedding.

"I'm being given a bachelor party on the second Wednesday evening before the wedding," James sighed.

"Oh my goodness," laughed Amy. "We're going to be partied out."

He pulled her into the office, giving her three kisses in a row. "My dearest Amy, we'll try to find some quiet time together in between for a concert or two, and a dinner by ourselves, with wedding talk forbidden. I will see to it that you don't get too overwhelmed by all this. That's a promise. Let's try to enjoy each day as it comes.

"Remember that we're having dinner at my house on Wednesday and then writing out the invitations."

"How could I forget? I'm picking up the invitations this afternoon, James dear."

Fenwick provided a delicious dinner for them and they stayed at the dining room table to write the invitations. Amy had typed a list of the names and addresses of the guests. Their wedding invitation read:

Amy Elizabeth Somerset
and
James Edward Carstairs

request the honour of your presence
at their wedding

on Saturday, December thirtieth
nineteen hundred and ninety-five

at twelve o'clock noon

St. Alban's Church

London

Reception and Luncheon following at Claridge's Hotel

R.S.V.P.

When the invitations were finally complete, they both had the same feeling of closure, as if announcing their wedding in writing somehow made it official. James kissed Amy tenderly and said: "You've made me so happy, my dear. I'm quite looking forward to giving up my bachelorhood."

"And I'm also looking forward to being married to you, dear James."

Amy was still very nervous about the weekend. She asked Barbara to come over to help her pack.

"Now Mother, James loves you, and that's what you have to remember. What can his sister do? It's too late; the invitations are in the mail."

"That's not any way to make me feel better, Barbara. If I know that I look my best, I'll have more courage. I'm getting my hair done at Giorgio's after work on Friday. Let's pick out some clothes now."

Barbara suggested taking a box of truffles or biscuits from Harrod's as a house gift.

"Thank you, Barbara. That's a wonderful idea. You've been a great help in easing my anxieties."

James picked Amy up promptly at ten on Saturday morning. As he put her suitcase in the car, he said: "Now dear, I know you're not looking forward to this weekend, but I promise I'll stay close to you and protect you. They are really a very nice couple, and I can assure you they'll be considerate and welcoming."

The day was sunny and just a bit cool, and since the drive took an hour and a half, they had plenty of time to talk. Of course, it was all about the wedding plans. They were to see the travel agent at noon on Tuesday, and James said that after the initial choice of their destination, he would like to take over and give her one less thing to think about. Also, he said that he didn't know how she felt about new luggage, but his was a disgrace.

Amy answered: "Well, you have seen mine. It's several years old and I only have two pieces."

They agreed to buy luggage for each other when they had the time.

Soon they were driving up the circular drive to his sister's house. It was quite large actually, a stone-and-brick two-storey with a columned portico.

Genevieve and Ian came to the door and greeted Amy and James with smiles, hugs and hearty congratulations.

"Please come in," said Ian. "I'm glad that the weather has finally warmed up a bit after that ghastly cold spell."

"Let's take your things up to your rooms and give you a few minutes before you come down for lunch," added Genevieve.

Lunch was served in the breakfast room with a warm fire blazing.

"How cozy this looks," remarked Amy with a smile.

"Sherry, everyone?" asked Ian.

"No thank you. Perhaps some tonic water," Amy replied.

"I'll have sherry," said James. "I need something to warm me up."

At lunch, they talked about plans for the wedding, but when James noticed Amy faltering a bit, he asked: "Ian, I would be honoured if you would agree to be my best man."

Ian stammered: "It would be my honour, James. Yes indeed."

James's sister added: "How thoughtful, James."

"We're having the wedding at St. Alban's Church near Amy's

flat, and the reception at Claridge's. We brought your invitation with us. We were determined to keep the guest list down to eighty, but it wasn't easy. I've reserved a room for you both at Claridge's for two or three nights, as we have a rehearsal on the Friday night. Could you come up to London next Saturday, Ian, to try on a tuxedo? If you have your own, we may still have to co-ordinate accessories. Afterwards, we men will get together for lunch at my club."

"Certainly, I'll come, James. Thank you."

"Who else is coming to the wedding, James?" asked Genevieve.

"Well, we have Lady Brocklehurst, a very old friend of Amy's grandmother, and Sir John and Lady Beaton, who are leasing her house, most members of the firm, many friends and some of the village residents of Ferndene who know Amy quite well and so on," replied James, with a wink at Amy.

"My matron of honour will be my daughter, Barbara, and my granddaughter, Stephanie, will be the flower girl. My son-in-law Jeffery and his son will help to usher, and my grandson will also be the ring-bearer."

"You certainly have done a lot of planning so far," exclaimed Genevieve.

"That's only the tip of the iceberg, Genevieve," James replied. "There's much more. Just thinking about it all is exhausting. We briefly considered eloping and I sometimes wonder if it wouldn't have been a good idea."

As they headed back to the living room, Genevieve mentioned to Amy that she had invited a few close friends in for dinner to meet them. Luckily, James had told Amy this, so she was prepared. Ian proudly showed them his conservatory, where he grew orchids as a hobby.

"I must tell you, Amy, that I have a pair of your lovely botanical drawings of orchids. I bought them years ago and just recently noticed again that you're the artist."

"That was a hobby of mine at one time and orchids were a favourite subject."

"My dear, you have so many talents," said Genevieve. "I would like to take a closer look at your beautiful ring. Did you choose it yourself, James?"

"Of course I did, Genevieve. I have some taste, but no experience of course."

"You must tell me how you proposed. Were you romantic, James? One does not know what to expect of a brother."

"Well, it was rather unusual, was it not, Amy?" He laughed and told them both about the balloon ascension first, and then about proposing on a picnic blanket.

"May we ask where you are going on your honeymoon?"

"We're flying to Barbados to stay for a whole month. It will be wonderful to have a long vacation," said James.

"Well, Amy, I can see that you have done wonders with James already. All for the better. We must change for dinner soon and I have a few other things to do." At that Genevieve gave Amy and James each a hug and congratulated them again.

"So far, so good," James whispered on the way upstairs.

Amy dressed carefully in her long black velvet skirt and white satin blouse. Madame Zolie had made her a reversible stole to wear with this. She wore her pearl earrings. Her hair shone as she patted her curls into place and put on a little scent. As she came out of her room, there was James waiting to escort her downstairs.

"My dear, you look extra beautiful tonight. If I hadn't asked you to marry me already, I would do it right now," and he kissed her tenderly on the cheek.

Voices could be heard in the front hall. As Amy and James came down the stairs, Genevieve and Ian met them, ready to introduce them to their first guests. Soon, there were others gathered in the living room, congratulating James and Amy, with James true to his promise to stay right beside Amy.

Talk flowed easily at dinner, everyone curious to know how they met, how he proposed and where they were going on their honeymoon. Some reminisced aloud about their own courtships and honeymoon trips.

Ian selected a fine champagne for a toast. It was a wonderful evening.

As they drove back to London on Sunday afternoon, Amy was very happy and said to James: "I didn't make a single mistake, did I dear? I'm so relieved."

James laughed in return. "Now my dear Amy, I don't know why you're so intimidated by my sister. I think it's quite the reverse now." He kissed her hand. "Our weekend turned out to be very good indeed."

At the office that week, James tried to keep their work lighter. He knew Amy was tired out, and didn't want her to come down with something.

On Tuesday, he took her for lunch and they bought new luggage together. They then went to the travel agent who arranged their airline tickets and recommended some first-rate hotels for their consideration. She also loaded them down with pamphlets about points of interest, car hires, etc. Since their passports were up-to-date, their travel plans seemed to be nearing completion.

The next evening, they met the kindly Vicar again. He approved of their music choices and said that the organist would be accompanied by a flautist. They went over their vows, which they had written together, and which also won the approval of the Vicar.

"I'm enjoying you two amazing people," he said. "Young people are so emotional and opinionated. I have quite a time with them occasionally."

On Saturday, James met the men as previously arranged, and Amy and the girls went to Madame Zolie's.

"Grandmother, wait until you see my dress! Madame Zolie is designing it just for me," exclaimed Stephanie, dancing with excitement. When she came out of the fitting room, she looked like a fairy princess. The dress was pale pink silk with rosebuds down the front to the waist, and a flared skirt. On her hair, which was swept up on the sides, Madame Zolie had pinned a matching long, flat bow.

As Stephanie approached them with shining eyes, Barbara, Georgina and Amy all exclaimed: "How perfectly lovely!"

"My darling Stephanie, you'll be the star," said Amy as she embraced her granddaughter.

Stephanie twirled around to show her flared skirt and told Grandmother gleefully: "Oh, I'm so happy. This is the most beautiful dress I've ever owned."

Everyone clapped and congratulated Madame Zolie, who beamed over another of her creations. The girls then went out to lunch. Stephanie was feeling very grown-up to be included.

Meanwhile, the men had gathered at the tuxedo shop. Under the manager's guidance, they chose their outfits. He suggested that James choose a more formal style rather than wear his traditional black tuxedo. Ian and Jeffery each owned a suitable tuxedo, so the manager suggested they choose different bow ties and cummerbunds—Ian in grey striped silk and Jeffery in plain grey. The tuxedo chosen for George was a miniature replica of his father's and he looked absolutely dashing in it. George couldn't stop smiling.

With their outfits settled, they took a taxi to James's club.

24

The weather had turned cooler in November. James picked Amy up at ten-thirty the next Saturday for the drive to Ferndene. He put her luggage in the car and as they drove out of the city, he remarked: "Aside from work, it's been a fairly quiet week for once. How are you feeling, Amy?"

"Well, now that our plans are mostly finalized, I feel much better. There are just several parties to get through now."

He kissed her hand and smiled: "Let's just try to enjoy them, my dear. Remember that we love each other, and people want to wish us well."

The Beatons congratulated them as they came in.

"We knew you two were going to get married eventually, did we not, Sir John?" gushed Lady Jane. "Yes indeed, you could not hide your feelings from us," he replied with a hearty laugh. "Your wedding's coming up soon too. We received your lovely invitation, and certainly plan to attend."

Tilly came out smiling and with a hug for both, said: "Congratulations. We didn't expect to be invited to the wedding, but we shall certainly come. Doctor and Mrs. Langford have invited us to drive with them."

Soon luncheon was served. The Beatons tried to keep the day peaceful and, after a light tea, sent them upstairs to prepare for the party.

Amy enjoyed a lovely hot bath and put on her navy taffeta skirt and cashmere sweater. Both felt very luxurious. Barbara had helped her to choose this outfit. Once more, when she came out of her room, James was waiting.

"I have certainly picked a most beautiful bride." He smiled and kissed her cheek and hand. They went downstairs together. The host and hostess were already in the living room.

"Might as well get you two a drink," said Sir John.

Others started to arrive—Vivian and Jim, Mr. and Mrs. Bromfield, Jane Barnaby and her husband, and to Amy's surprise, Mr. and Mrs. Epsom-Smythe, she clad in a black velvet dress and pearls. Mrs. Epsom-Smythe assumed a quieter more genteel voice appropriate to the occasion. Her husband was a quiet, balding, short man.

It was a wonderful gathering. Amy was pleased to see her old neighbours again and to have the opportunity to introduce her future husband to those who had not met him.

Amy and James were presented with monogrammed sheets and towels by the group. They thanked the Beatons and the other guests for the thoughtful gift.

The party didn't break up until late because they were all enjoying themselves so much. They all had been invited to the wedding and each one mentioned that they were looking forward to the occasion. The Beatons took this opportunity to inform Amy and James that they were going on a Mediterranean cruise in mid-April and moving back into London immediately on their return.

As they drove away from Bower House the next day, Amy enthused over how she had enjoyed the party. "The house will be ours in May, James. I hope that you'll come to share my love of it. I do believe that the Beatons came to enjoy it and will be sad to leave."

On the way home, they discussed their future plans and decided that they both would retire at the end of April. James kissed Amy with affection as she prepared to get out of the car, not noticing Mrs. Fillmore smiling from behind the curtains.

The partners and their wives held a party in their honour at a private club on the following Wednesday night. There were jokes about James the confirmed bachelor being caught at last and congratulations to them both. Amy knew most of the partners and their wives from earlier years as William's wife. This thought upset her for a few moments, but James, seeing her face, read her thoughts and squeezed her hand and held her close.

"Come Amy, this is our party."

She smiled back, feeling comfort in his reassurance. There were numerous toasts to their upcoming wedding. Everyone was obviously very happy for them. Once again, the women exclaimed over her beautiful ring and all wanted to know about their honeymoon plans. The firm presented Amy and James with a set of Waterford crystal goblets, twelve of each, for wine and sherry. James was the senior partner after all.

The secretaries had set a date for a luncheon party for Amy. The cafeteria was cheerfully decorated with crepe paper and wedding bells. A large cake was the centrepiece. Of course, all of the girls had to see her ring again. There was much chatter and laughter. Everyone was so happy for her. They presented her with a crystal sherry decanter.

Josie came up to her after and said: "Amy, I feel so pleased for you. I've taken your advice and have been getting out quite often. In fact, I've been seeing a young man from the choir at our church. We have much in common and he makes me laugh again."

All of their arrangements were nearing finalization. James and Amy, Barbara and Jeffery and Basil and Georgina decided to meet at Claridge's for lunch one day to view the reception rooms and to discuss menus and other arrangements. The staff was most helpful and offered many suggestions for their consideration. The menu was settled and Barbara and Georgina promised to take care of the seating arrangements.

"Thank you so much everyone. I think I can speak on Amy's behalf too on having such wonderful friends and family to help us to make our wedding day most memorable," James said with sincerity.

"Oh yes, my dears," added Amy with tears in her eyes. "You are indeed good to us."

James had a bachelor dinner given for him at his club by his close friends and associates. The men made sport of his long bachelorhood coming to an end, but were sincere in wishing him and Amy much happiness.

Barbara and Jeffery moved Amy's belongings from her flat into their house a week before the wedding. James insisted on Amy bringing most of her knick-knacks to his house, soon to be hers too. Her painting was hung beside his over the mantelpiece making a most tasteful arrangement.

"We'll also have to find a special place for your botanical drawings," he remarked proudly.

Christmas seemed a minor affair with the wedding following so closely. The celebration was held at Barbara and Jeffery's home. They enjoyed a traditional Christmas dinner with all the trimmings. Of course, James was included as a member of Amy's family and he thoroughly enjoyed this new role of belonging.

Barbara helped Amy to organize her wardrobe and pack her new luggage for the honeymoon. She carefully packed the beautiful lacy silk shawl given to Amy by Madame Zolie as a bridal gift.

The rehearsal went well on Friday evening. Stephanie pretended she was scattering rose petals out of a basket before the bride. The Vicar seemed very pleased and, as he gave clear instructions, it only took one run-through for them all to know their duties. The rehearsal dinner was enjoyed at a nearby restaurant.

James and Amy were very happy and relieved to have the preparations behind them. They looked into each other's eyes with deep love. All seemed ready. They just had to wait for tomorrow and the wedding.

25

The day dawned with abundant sunshine filling the cool air. Everyone was up early—too excited for sleep. The ladies went to have their hair done and their nails manicured. Giorgio served them sweet rolls and coffee. He was as excited as they were. They looked beautiful, and Giorgio commented that the three generations—Amy, Barbara and Stephanie—resembled one another so closely.

"What a beautiful family!" he said with enthusiasm. "Congratulations again, Madame. I wish you many happy years."

They then hurried home to Barbara's house where they were to dress. Jeffery and George went to James's, as did Ian. Limousines had been hired for them all, and they were ready in plenty of time.

As Amy finished dressing, Barbara said: "Mother, you look so radiant and happy. You're marrying a man who will take care of you for the rest of your life and will love you forever." She gave her a kiss.

Just then Stephanie burst in: "Hurry everyone, the limousine is here." She looked so delightful. Grandmother and mother were very proud.

"Don't we look smashing?" said Stephanie.

The men of the wedding party had arrived at the church early. When the ladies arrived, Barbara helped her mother out of the limousine and Georgina too. Stephanie bounded out with no assistance. As it was a cool day, they hurried in and left their wraps at the back of the church. The florist met the ladies at the door and gave each her flowers.

The lovely old church simply glowed, with sunlight streaming through the stained-glass windows giving added colour to the beautiful floral arrangements. The effect could only be described as spectacular.

Jeffery and George, looking handsome in their tuxedoes, had conducted all of the guests to their places. George was beaming with pride and was truly gallant in offering his arm to each lady in turn.

Barbara walked up the aisle slowly as the music began, followed by George with the rings, and by Stephanie strewing pink rose petals. Jeffery took Amy's arm and said with a smile: "Our turn, Amy."

As they walked up the aisle to the soaring music of the organ, Amy focussed on just one thing—James's loving, smiling eyes. Jeffery handed Amy to James who grasped her hand tightly. Stephanie stood beside Barbara, and George beside Ian.

A hush fell over the congregation as the kindly Vicar intoned the words that would make them man and wife. George came carefully forward with the rings. James slipped a three-diamond wedding band on Amy's finger as he spoke the vows that they had composed together. Amy then slipped a gold and platinum band on James's finger, speaking the same words in a clear and sure voice.

As they were pronounced man and wife, James embraced her and kissed her tenderly and whispered: "I love you, Mrs. Carstairs."

They turned and walked arm-in-arm down the aisle meeting the smiles of their family and friends as the music soared once again.

26

The wedding reception at Claridge's was a huge success. There were many toasts, and everyone expressed heart-felt best wishes to this wonderful couple.

The flowers, decorations and food were exceptional.

The children were delighted to be included in this happy event and were proud to be seated at the head table. Genevieve, James's sister, was awed by some of the guests. Lady Brocklehurst, Sir John and Lady Beaton sat together with Jim and Vivian and the Bromfields. Tilly and Walter sat with the Fillmores. Mrs. Fillmore wore a large plumed hat, which threatened to poke an eye out of anyone who came within range. They were joined by the Epsom-Smythes and the Barnabys.

The reception and luncheon went on for nearly three hours. Finally, James and Amy slipped out for a few minutes to change. Barbara helped Amy to dress. As they came down the broad stairs, the guests were waiting, and they showered confetti on James and Amy on their way to the limousine.

James and Amy took a moment to hug and kiss Stephanie

and George and to thank them for the important roles that they had played in the wedding. They also promised to send post-cards to them from Barbados.

In the car, James kissed Amy many times and repeatedly called her Mrs. Carstairs.

"What a wonderful name," she said, "Amy Carstairs."

"Tomorrow, we head to Barbados, my dear Amy. May this be the beginning of many, many adventures together."